KAY CASTANEDA

Emmie of Indianapolis

The Story of an American Girl

Bookplaces

PUBLISHING

"My name is Emmie, and I want to tell you what happened to me when I was twelve years old. Mother told us she was getting a divorce from our father, and she was taking my sisters and me away. Some people said that I was too old to be calling her Mommy, but I didn't care.
I loved her so much."
Emmie O'Brien

"Look back and smile on perils past."

WALTER SCOTT

Contents

Foreword

I wrote this story in order to preserve the history of a city, its people, neighborhoods and culture for future generations. When I told stories about my experiences growing up in the 1960s in Indianapolis, I received many remarks. What? I don't remember anything like that happening! I have nothing to remember. Why should I remember? I grew up in the suburbs, they said. I lived in a small town, or out in the country, others replied. That's for old people, all that remembering stuff, they said. I disagree.

Soldier's and Sailors Monument, Indianapolis, Indiana by Kay Castaneda

Preface

In my dream, I saw a man wearing a white robe starting to ascend
the stairs, and I ran after him. Are you Jesus, I asked? I am
John the Evangelist. Write! Write now, he replied. What do you
want me to write about, I asked again.
The little girl, he answered, write about the little girl. Then
he was gone, and I saw a young girl wearing white, standing in
the middle of a crossroads where many streets met in the center.
I remember her, I said. Her name was Emmie. I will write about
her.

One

Take the Long Way Home

ndianapolis, Indiana 1963

I STORMED OUT OF MY room and jerked the front door open when I heard her say that, fast as my legs could run down the block. I cut through the backyards, over old man Henry's pepper plants, squashing most of them when I slipped in the dirt. He screamed something dirty to me from his window, something like idiot little rat, but I wasn't sure. Mrs. Apple let me in her kitchen after I rattled the screen door.

"Hurry! That damn fat monster's after me!"

"What? That kind of language isn't like you at all. What's the matter? The kids are with their grandmother, Emmie. Why don't you stay and have a pancake?"

I sat down at the table while she served me little pancakes filled with raisins and nuts.

"You need twelve for the plate to look good."

And they did look good with all the butter she piled on top of them. As she poured the syrup over each one, I told her how pretty they were. Mrs. Apple really cared about the appearance of her food. When all my little pancakes were gone, she brought me hot cocoa. Old man Henry snuck up to the door, and I jumped out of my seat.

"Where is that delinquent? She needs a good whippin' and I'll do it."

Mrs. Apple met him at the door and threatened to call the police. I felt safe then.

"Can I read now?"

Mrs. Apple always let me pick any book from the shelves in her living room to read. But all I wanted to do was find the word "divorce" in the dictionary. As I searched through the letter "d" words, I found what I was looking for. Divorce—a severing of ties between a husband and wife. I didn't know what severing meant, so I looked up that word also. I kept on reading, but Mrs. Apple's children never came home.

"See you later, Mrs. Apple."

"Goodbye, Emmie. Come back and visit me again."

Mommy saw me wandering down the street, so she hollered to me.

"Come inside, honey, I have something to tell you."

I took my time getting back in the house. My little sisters were lined up side by side on the living room couch. Little Cissy kept leaning her head over on Janey's arm. I sat down beside them and crossed my knees.

"Girls, we're moving to another house on Saturday. Your Daddy and I are getting a divorce."

Mommy looked straight at us, puffing deep on her Pall Mall, waiting for me or my sisters to answer her. I looked sideways at the two of them, but they didn't move. There was not a sound in the room. I felt as if somebody ought to say something, so I spoke up.

"Oh!" Why? Don't you love Daddy anymore?"

Mommy kept staring at us, but she didn't answer.

"That means you'll have to pack all your toys and clothes in a big cardboard box. You get busy now."

Cissy climbed down from the couch and came over to me. The three of us walked into the bedroom and left Mommy still smoking her cigarette. I made sure that we put Cissy's things in first because I knew she'd have a crying fit if we forgot anything. Janey took all her clothes from the drawers and dumped them down into the box. Then she sat on the floor next to Cissy while I packed my comic books and skates. My school uniform went on top of everything and last, our winter coats.

"We're done now, Mommy!"

Janey ran into the kitchen where our mother was standing on a chair throwing pots and pans into a box. Mommy made a lot of noise all evening, and the smoke from her cigarettes was so thick it choked me. There was nothing else to do. My sisters and I watched *Gunsmoke* until it was time for bed. Early on Saturday morning, I ran around to the neighbors to let them know I was leaving. Every one of them asked me why.

"It's because of the divorce," I answered as I hugged everybody goodbye.

Some neighbors patted me on the head or gave me a kiss. Mrs. Apple grabbed a coffee cake from her counter that she had just finished baking. It was all wrapped up in wax paper on a tray when she gave it to me.

"You poor child. Take this and keep the tray. Now, who is going to come and eat my food? Give your little sisters some of that cake. It's cinnamon pecan. God bless you!"

"Thank you, Mrs. Apple. I'm sorry that I can't come over to eat here anymore. Goodbye!"

I ran back home carrying the coffee cake close to my chest. It was still warm when I put it down on the table. Mommy was drinking a cup of coffee. I cut her a slice of cake and one for me. We sat facing each other across the table.

"Could I drink coffee too, Mommy? It's a coffee cake. Mrs. Apple gave it to us."

Mommy reached over and took a clean cup from the box. She filled my cup from the percolator and handed me a spoon.

"I suppose you can have a cup. It's moving day."

We ate cake together and drank coffee. The second hand on the clock ticked loudly while Mommy and I had breakfast. It was quiet in the house for a while until Cissy woke up. She jumped up and down on her bed crying for me to hold her. I couldn't do it. My throat was tight, and my arms felt too light to hold anyone. Mommy reminded me of moving as I went out the back door.

3

"Don't get lost, Emmie. We'll be leaving in a few hours."

I knew where to go, to my secret tree where no one could find me. At the edge of my neighborhood, there was a big piece of land without any houses in a wooded area with many tall trees. I followed my path around the last yard, over a cement pipe that crossed the creek. My tree was in the middle of all the other trees, but it was the best one with a round trunk and no ugly spots on the bark. The arms of my tree stretched up almost straight just like a person would raise their arms toward heaven. All it took was one foot on the side to push myself up, and I was sitting in my seat between the arms. I pretended that the tree had a lap. It was a living tree just like the ones in *The Wizard of Oz*. Mine was a good tree. I was protected if anything evil tried to get me. There were no fruit or nuts on my tree, so when my enemies came for me, my tree would pick up rocks and throw them at the bad people. A family of cardinals lived in my tree. The mother was plain, but she always stayed with her husband. He was bright red and very flashy. They brought back worms and food for their babies, never minding if I was there. I picked two leaves and pressed them over my eyes. When I looked straight up at the sun, I could see the veins inside the leaves. Down below, the water in the creek flowed and bubbled over the rocks while I was sleeping. I could hear my father's voice before I saw him. I let him get closer and closer to me before I said anything. Then he was standing directly below me. I looked down and saw the part in the top of his hair.

"Here I am, Daddy! Up here in the tree!"

When he raised his arms up to me, I jumped. I was small for my age. He stumbled a bit, but we didn't fall.

"Your mother's looking for you. Let's go now."

We walked slowly back home, his hand on my shoulder. The station wagon was loaded up with all our boxes. Little Cissy was sitting on the sidewalk watching Janey do cartwheels on the lawn.

"Wait! I can't forget Teddy!"

I ran back into the house and searched all the rooms. There he was, sitting on the floor of my closet. Teddy was my six-foot-tall stuffed bear that I'd won at the fair when I was ten. I still liked to keep him in my room. I came dragging him out by the arms, stumbling down the steps.

"We don't have room for that thing, Emmie. Get in now. Bring your sisters and let's go."

Mommy was sitting behind the steering wheel. She puffed hard on her cigarette and blew the smoke toward Daddy's face. I could not make my sisters mind me no matter what I said, so Daddy put both of them in the back seat. I was the last one to get in the car, still holding Teddy.

"Alright. You can take him. But you'll have to sit on him all the way."

Mommy gave in and slammed the car door shut. She turned the key, and the radio came on as Johnny Cash sang *Ring of Fire*. We drove away from our house. Daddy kept standing there on the front sidewalk, waving at us. I saw him when I turned my head around and looked out the back window. He kept getting smaller and smaller until I couldn't see him anymore. When we turned the corner, he was completely gone.

Two

When the Angels Arrive

W e left our house in Lawrence, Indiana with the furniture still in place, curtains hanging and the pictures up on the walls. The day seemed like one time when my family went on vacation to another city. The buildings all looked old and strange. Big houses with tall windows lined every street. Every house had something to fascinate me; porches wrapping all around the front and sides, towers with pointed roofs and circle windows. Some houses had stone lions guarding their entrances. Others were covered with wooden shingles and ivy outside. There were homes that had thick front doors and stained glass with yellow, red and blue. I could see pictures of birds and angels and flowers in the windows and doors. Some of the houses had small windows at the very top. As we drove by, I named all the different shapes to Janey and Cissy.

"Diamond, triangle, oblong, square, rectangle, heart, circle, oval."

Mommy drove and drove around the entire neighborhood.

"Are we in Cincinnati?" I asked her.

"No, honey, we're in Indianapolis. Lawrence is a part of Indianapolis, on the east side. This is the center of the city. Now we'll get an apartment here soon as I can find one."

Janey kept pushing me over to the side of the car door, but I didn't say anything. I was too busy looking out the window at everything as we passed by. What huge houses and little yards! They were so close together. You could lean out one window and touch the window of the house next door. Where would my sisters and I play outside? The yards were only big enough to stand in.

Mommy drove the station wagon slowly up and down each street until we stopped in the area of 16th and Pennsylvania Street. She had a newspaper on the seat beside her. We were parked in front of a drugstore on the corner. Mommy read the newspaper for a while and smoked another cigarette. I wanted to go inside the drugstore because I could see people sitting at the counter eating sandwiches.

"When are we getting lunch? It's one o'clock now."

"Emmie, we have to move into our apartment first. Be quiet and wait. I have to find Talbot Street."

The people at the counter stirred cream and sugar into their coffee and stared back out at me. I looked in all directions to find the street.

"Look! Mommy, there's a sign across the street. It says Talbot."

The house with our apartment was tall and white with three stories and a huge front porch. We waited in the station wagon while Mommy went inside to rent our new apartment.

"Help me carry Cissy inside while I get some of our things. This place is only fifteen dollars a week, and it has furniture."

I carried the baby upstairs, but Janey just followed me. She was only seven years old, but she hung on to me too much.

"Janey, get your blanket and bring it in."

I laid Cissy on the sofa. It looked scratchy and old with holes on the arms, and it was an ugly dark brown. We had the apartment in the front of the house on the second floor. I looked out the window and saw Mommy down on the sidewalk talking to a man. Soon I heard them coming up the stairs. He came in first and carried the boxes into the bedroom. Mommy helped him set up Cissy's playpen in the living room by the window. I remembered

I left Teddy down in the car alone. It was such a heavy bear that I had to push him up the stairs. When I reached the landing, I lay down on the floor and shoved Teddy with my feet into the apartment.

"God Almighty! What kind of a thing is that?"

It was the landlord. He had such a big loud voice that he woke up Cissy.

"Listen, you! You better not tear up my property. You hear me?"

The old man yelled right at us as he shook his fist. I grabbed Cissy while Mommy struck a match and lit her cigarette. She told him that we were good kids and that we would not destroy anything that belonged to him. We'd keep our apartment clean, and not bother anyone.

"I hope that darn baby don't cry all night, either. Your rent is due again next Saturday. I'll be here at noon to collect."

He slammed the door. We could hear his feet hit each step on the way down until he went out the front door mumbling.

"What a mean old man. What an ogre!"

Mommy crushed her cigarette in the ashtray and began to cry. After that, we always called the landlord Mr. Ogre, but not to his face. We could see him down in front, sweeping the sidewalk or working on his car. Janey stuck out her tongue as she looked down on him. Once, she spit out the window, but it did not hit Mr. Ogre. The spit just ran down the front shingles and glistened in the sun for a few hours. When we saw him, we didn't say anything since he might yell or come after us kids.

I helped Mommy unpack our dishes. Janey kept quiet, but we made her take all her clothes out of the box and put them in the dresser. Janey and I each had a uniform from our Catholic school. There was no Catholic school nearby, so we hung the blue plaid jumpers and other skirts up in the back of the closet. The room where Janey and I slept had a small bed pushed up against the wall. Janey lined up my roller skates and her dolls on the windowsill. I stacked my books and my school supplies on top of the dresser. It was a different kind of bedroom than we had out in the suburbs. This room had gray wallpaper covered with giant purple roses, and the window reached from the ceiling almost to the floor. We didn't have white lace curtains like my old room. Now, we only had a paper shade with a tear in the middle. I pulled the string, and the shade rolled up around the tube. I watched it spin so fast that dust blew down on my face and made me sneeze.

"Look, Mommy. Come and see our new room."

Janey yelled for Mommy down the hallway. The bed was already covered with sheets. They were stiff, but they weren't dirty. Janey spread her blue blanket over the bed and propped her stuffed cat on the pillow.

"It's great, Janey" Mommy told her.

"Where are you and Cissy going to sleep?"

"In the living room. I'll sleep on the couch and Cissy will have to sleep in her playpen."

We continued to make the apartment into our new home. Mommy went out to the store and came back with food for our supper. She tried the new stove and cooked minute steaks and baked potatoes. The kitchen had such a tiny table, red metal with red plastic chairs. We kept bumping elbows as we ate. Cissy didn't even sit down. She walked around with a piece of steak in her hand and got a bite of potato and corn from the rest of us.

"Could I wash the dishes now, Mommy?"

I always liked how the soapy water felt. I took a rag and washed the entire room, the refrigerator, stove, windows and the floor. In the living room, there was a big pole that connected the ceiling to the floor. It was right out in the middle of the linoleum. Cissy and Janey were trying to wrap their arms around it, but they couldn't do it. Then I tried, and I wasn't able to either. Mommy almost did it, but she gave up. The pole was so wide that Mommy could stand on one side of it, and we couldn't see any part of her body. We played hide and seek for a while until I remembered about Sammy Terry. He had a good show every week. I thought it was funny that he dressed up in a long black robe and wore makeup like a dead person. We were lucky that Daddy had put our television in the back of the station wagon. Mommy got one of our new neighbors to carry it up the stairs. Mr. Hubert was very tall and thin. He lived downstairs beneath us. He grunted a little when he placed the television on the metal TV stand, but he was very friendly. Mommy offered to give him a tip, but he wouldn't take it. With a wink at Janey, he left.

"Come down and get me anytime you girls need help. I'm a widower!"

I thought that meant some type of religion, but Mommy explained that it meant he wasn't married since his wife was dead.

"Why did his wife die? Why does he live alone? Does he have any children? Do you think he gets lonely down there? Why doesn't he get married again?"

"Stop, Emmie. I don't know! Maybe you should go and interview him."

I knew what an interview was. Movie stars were often interviewed for magazines. Reporters interviewed criminals for the newspaper. I thought for a long time about how I could interview Mr. Hubert. I would knock on his door and ask him if he would answer some questions for me. I would need new paper for my three-ring binder to take notes about his answers. While I was thinking, Mommy made chocolate pudding for Janey and me and a warm bottle of milk for the baby. We sat on the couch with the pole in front of us and ate our dessert. Janey had to sit way on the other side away from me if she wanted to see the television. Cissy drank all the milk from her bottle and went to sleep. Mommy sat at the kitchen table and read her True Story magazine until late at night. *Invasion of the Body Snatchers* was on Sammy Terry's Nightmare Theater. I had to explain everything to Janey. She would come over to my side of the couch, whisper a question, and then go back to her side. Mommy woke us up when the television screen was gray and giving off a buzzing sound of the sign-off. We had stayed up until all the programs went off the air. Then Janey and I slept in our new bedroom. The light from the moon came through the hole in the shade. It made a halo of light all around Teddy in the corner. I could see him watching me and smiling as I went to sleep.

Three

Somewhere Over the Rainbow

S unday morning, I went outside while everyone was sleeping. My new neighborhood did not look so bad after all. On the corner by our apartment, there was a bowling alley and grill. I tried to look through the windows, but all I could see was the floor. Shiny wooden planks stretched out as far as I could see to the rear of the building. There was a sign on the front door.

WALLY'S BOWL & LUNCH-BURGERS, EGGS & STEW

CLOSED SUNDAY OPEN MON-SAT 9:00 A.M.-10:00 P.M.

I knew that I would come back in the morning as soon as I woke up. 22nd was the next street I came to. More businesses lined the street, a meat market, a hardware store and a Laundromat. Small shops were at almost every corner in the neighborhood, but they weren't open on Sundays either. Next, I walked until I reached a large, brick building on the corner of 16th and Pennsylvania Street. I stood on the front steps to read the door.

JOHN HERRON ART INSTITUTE & MUSEUM

OPEN MONDAY-FRIDAY 10:00 AM-5:00 PM

How nice, my own museum so close to my apartment. I could go every day, but it was also closed on Sunday. I knew that my family and I were supposed to be at Mass. But where was the Catholic Church? I looked up and down the streets, searching for a statue of a saint or familiar names such as Our Lady, Holy, Saint or Blessed. Mommy said we would go to a new Catholic Church here as soon as we were settled. Now all I saw was a sign painted on the plate glass window of a little store.

CHURCH OF DELIVERANCE & HOUSE OF THE LORD

We couldn't go to that church. It looked small, and there were no words in the name that I recognized. Did they have fountains with holy water near the door? Maybe their saints were inside. I wondered if they had a big cross hanging above the altar. Getting closer, I could read the smaller letters at the bottom of the window.

ALL ARE WELCOME!

I began to hear singing coming from inside the store. A great crowd of voices joined together in a joyful tune.

"Oh, welcome to the house of the Lord, our Savior. Welcome to the place of joy. God our Father is good and righteous. Thanks be to Him on high!"

The door was open since it was a warm July day. All the women inside had on big, beautiful hats with all kinds of flowers. One lady even had peacock feathers sticking straight up from the band of her hat. Some of the hats had pieces of see-through material hanging down to their eyes. The ladies cooled themselves with little paper fans printed with Bible verses and pictures of doves. All the colors matched. If a woman had on a lavender dress, she wore a lavender hat. Some of the women had on shoes the same color as the rest of their outfits. One woman wore a pale rose-colored dress with tiny white dots and a matching hat and shoes. Even her purse was covered in the same fabric as the rest of her clothing. They all had on white gloves, even the little girls.

I kept watching one woman who was wearing a light blue dress and a hat covered with white pearls. Her pearl necklace and earrings matched the pearls of the hat. I started to count the pearls on the hat when she began to sing alone. She swayed back and forth, raising her arms up in front of her. It was a deep and serious tune, and her words kept hold of my mind. It was something about a bridge and a river, and all who crossed it were never the same. I tried to understand what she was singing about, and then at the end of the song, she stretched out the words "Oh, Lord!" that I thought she would go on singing all morning. Then she yelled out "Amen! Praise the Lord! Hallelujah!"

I stood in the doorway listening and watching. Suddenly, the lady in the blue dress with the pearl hat saw me and ran over to meet me. She grabbed both my hands and pulled me in the door. My hands looked so little and white compared to her big dark hands. I noticed that she had a pearl ring to match all the other pearls of her outfit. The lady pushed me down in a chair marked Visitor on the back. There I was sitting right between two women who each had a beautiful hat. I didn't have a hat on. I looked down at myself with my jean shorts and a white shirt tied in a knot above my belly button. I was wearing my old navy blue sneakers, and I wasn't wearing any socks. Then all of the sudden, I felt as if my head was glowing. The sunshine came straight down on my redhead, and I became aware of how much different I was. How I wished that I had a beautiful pink or blue hat with a flower on it. Maybe a yellow lace dress like the little girl wore who sat in front of me. I looked around. The sun ray was only shining down on me. But the people were not laughing at me. Instead, they smiled and prayed "Amen, Amen, Amen!" The preacher got up and talked about heaven and how one day soon everyone in that room would get to go see the Lord. He kept talking loudly, hitting the side of his leg with one hand, and raising his Bible up straight in the air with the other. When the people all stood up to sing a song, I copied them. I clapped my hands and sang Amen! They passed around the collection basket, but I had no money to put in it. The lady with the blue dress handed me a dime.

"Here, darlin'. This is yours to keep or to give to Our Savior."

I dropped the coin down into the basket and tapped the girl in front of me on the shoulder. She turned around and smiled so friendly as she took the money basket from me. That big sunbeam shone on me the whole hour. It followed me out the door where the lady in the blue dress squeezed me hard.

"Come back, little angel darling, to the House of the Lord."

I couldn't think of very much to say. All the colors were blinding me, and my head was dizzy from all the singing and clapping.

"See you later. The music was pretty!"

Then I ran around the corner, and that sunbeam was still after me. It was still blinding me. The whole street was lit up as I ran back home.

"Wake up Janey. Look, Cissy! There's a light from the House of the Lord."

My sisters and I looked out the window at a beautiful rainbow. It stretched over the housetops and the colors were like the women's hats in church that morning. The sun was yellow like that girl's lace dress. All the stained glass windows on the block were sparkling. This was going to be a different kind of place to live.

Four

Down on Main Street

School was out before we moved to the new neighborhood. On Monday, Mommy sent me to the meat market.

"You can go shopping, Emmie. You know where everything is around here."

I pushed open the screen door of the market on the corner and went inside. The man behind the case saw me immediately.

"What can I get for you?"

He had a strange sounding voice. Maybe he was from a different state, not Indiana.

"Little girl! What can I do for you?"

I kept hearing the sound of his voice, but since it was unusual, I couldn't speak up right away.

"One pound of hamburger" I managed to say.

"Take a minute, girl."

He chose a piece of meat from his case with the glass window. I watched as he squeezed it down into the metal grinder and turned the handle again and again. The chopped meat came out of a tube with holes on the side of the grinder and landed on a sheet of brown paper. He stopped grinding and placed the paper with the meat on a scale. The black needle on the dial pointed to just past a half pound. So he turned the crank a few more times. He carried the paper with the rest of the meat back to the scale. It was one pound of hamburger. When he reached over to tear off a piece of tape, that's when I saw the blue numbers on his arm. I could see six or seven numbers just under the edge of his shirtsleeve. It looked like they were painted on his skin, but the paint had never washed off. He taped the package of meat and wrote the price on the outside with a black pen. Then his sleeve covered the numbers, and I couldn't read them anymore.

"Forty-nine cents. You be a good customer now little girl."

He leaned over the counter and dropped the package into my hands. He was a nice looking man with dark hair and eyes, sort of like Daddy, but his skin was a little darker. But those numbers, they were the thing that I saw the most. They were deep blue letters, and they kept getting bigger and darker until all I could see were numbers everywhere. I looked at my arm. I had no numbers painted on it, and there were no numbers on Janey or Cissy. I had never seen anybody with painted numbers. Why didn't he wash them off? Why did he seem to cover them but not to hide them? I could open my mouth and ask Why did you paint numbers on your arm? I was afraid of his answer.

"Pay the lady."

Then the numbers began to fade from my view, and the room seemed like a store again.

"Thank you."

I smiled at the man behind the meat case and turned around.

"I am Mrs. Steinbaum. You are new around this neighborhood?"

"Yes. I just moved here on Saturday."

Mrs. Steinbaum had a different sounding voice also, but hers was not as strange as her husband's voice. I watched her push the number four key on her wooden cash register and then the number nine. She picked up a chart that was suspended from the register by a chain and consulted it for the correct amount of tax. She pushed another button and then the total key. In the window of the cash register, a little white tag popped up that read SALE. I jumped back when the bell rang, it was so loud. I was just leaving when Mr.

16

Steinbaum called me over.

"Gum for little girls."

I reached into the glass jar he offered me and pulled out a black ball. I grabbed a red one for Janey.

"Licorice gum. You like it."

They both waved at me when I left the store. Mommy made Sloppy Joes for supper, Janey's favorite. We sat outside on the porch after we ate. Mrs. Ogre, our landlord's wife, asked Mommy lots of questions.

"Why are you divorced? Where is your husband? When are you going to get a job?"

Mommy couldn't stand it anymore, so we went for a walk. There was a little tavern two blocks from our apartment.

MULLIGAN'S BAR LIQUOR & POOL CLOSED SUNDAY

Mommy stopped at the door and told us to wait.

"I'm going to get a job here. Be still."

I sat down on the sidewalk with Janey and Cissy. Mommy came out and said she was going to be a waitress at night.

"What is a waitress?" Janey wanted to know.

"I serve drinks, and the people pay me tips. Emmie, you will have to babysit while I'm

gone."

"What if someone bad comes over?"

"They won't. Lock the door."

Five

Don't Worry Baby

I t was hot the first night Mommy went to work at the tavern. All our windows were open, but no air came inside. I let Cissy be naked, and Janey wore her shorty gown. I had to stay dressed until Mommy got back home. We watched television until it was late. Janey began whining.

"When's Mommy coming home?"

I made her sit beside me on the sofa until she felt safer. We were lying there with the sound on the television real low because we were afraid to wake up Mr. Ogre downstairs. The detective in the movie was trying to find a woman who ran away from home. We had all the lights off because Mr. Ogre said that we used too much electricity and that we shouldn't turn on too many lamps. The detective was talking very low to a man in a store, and then I suddenly noticed that someone real was standing by the side of the couch. I looked up to see a big man standing over us. We didn't notice when he came in because we were interested in the movie. His eyes were so big that they seemed to be coming out of his face. He made a grunting sound like a wild animal and reached for us. I screamed and jumped over Janey on the couch. The broom was standing in the corner by the stove, and I grabbed it. I hit him right in the middle of the head with the handle. I hit his big hands, and I stuck the broom straw in his face. He stopped reaching for Janey and turned around after me. Then he put his hands up to his eyes and started screaming. The light from the television was bright during a commercial for Spic and Span. Blood began to drip from the man's head, down his cheek, and onto the linoleum. I smelled the stink of rotten wine.

"AH AH AH AH"

He screamed and rubbed the blood all over his giant's face. When he turned and went out into the hallway, one of his hands smeared blood on the wall. I still had my broom, so I pushed him out the apartment door. He stumbled on the landing and rolled down the stairs, smearing more blood on the steps and rail. All the way down, he moaned like some wild beast, a strange type of animal, not a man. His voice echoed up to me at the top of the stairs as I held the broom.

"You can't run away, ever! I know where you live. I'll get you, young girl!"

I stood there on the landing looking down at all the blood. There was no light, just the light from the television in our apartment. Music from a jazz band played in the movie. I could hear the detective ask questions to the bartender as he ordered a beer. Then Mr. Hubert, our other neighbor downstairs, appeared in the doorway.

"Is everything okay, girls? I just got in from my night job, and I saw that this outer door was open. You need anything?"

The blood glistened and sparkled. It covered my eyes, and I could not see anything else.

"I say, you need anything?"

Slowly, the blood dried and faded from my view. I guess Mr. Hubert couldn't see it from down at the bottom of the steps.

"I'm just cleaning until Mommy gets home. She'll be here at midnight."

Mr. Hubert shook his head and backed away from the entry.

"You be careful now. There's evil all around."

I ran down the stairs and locked the outside door to the hallway. Next, I pushed the kitchen table in front of our apartment door and put the broom on top of it. If anyone tried to open the door, they'd make a lot of noise, and I would surely hear them before they got to my sisters and me. Over in the playpen, my little naked Cissy slept. I woke her up to see whether she was still alive. I put a clean diaper on her and rubbed powder on her neck where she was sweating. I took her to bed with Janey and me. Teddy slept at the foot of the bed. It was crowded, but I didn't care. In the middle of the night, Mommy came home from work. I had to scoot the table away from the door to let her inside. When she heard what happened, she said that I would have to sleep with a knife by my bed. There was no money for a babysitter. I would have to be on guard with a weapon all the time. Next morning, I again saw the blood on the walls.

"I killed him!"

I woke everybody up. Mommy told me that I just hurt the man, but I was sure that he was dead. I took a rag and a dishpan full of suds, and I washed all the blood that I could see. I scrubbed the floor, then the handrail. His big fingerprints disappeared when I rubbed them with the rag. I washed each step and the walls in the hallway. When I got to the main door downstairs, Mr. Ogre saw me. I smiled at him and kept scrubbing the brass doorknob until it shined. I cleaned the stained glass and then shook out the front mat. With my broom, I swept the entire front porch, the steps and the sidewalk in front of the house. Mr. and Mrs. Ogre peeped out the front window at me. I could feel them staring at me as I kept working. He had such a loud voice that I could hear him when he talked about me to his wife.

"That sure is a real weird kid. She's always cleaning or sweeping something. Don't act like any kid I ever known."

When I was done, Mommy told me to take a bath with dish powder. It made lots of suds up to the top of the tub. I scrubbed my hands real hard and examined them closely for blood. Did any of his blood get inside of me? When were the police coming to take me to jail? I soaked for a long time and slid under the water, holding my breath. I put more powder on my hair and made bubbles. Then I dipped my head back under the water again. When I climbed out, I combed my hair. How straight it was and long. I'd have to wait until it was dry to make my braid. I practiced making faces in the mirror.

"I'm innocent, Judge! It was an accident!"

And the most convincing plea, I thought, "I didn't mean to do it!" I thought about all the police shows I watched and how the murderers are led down a long hall toward their cell. The guard opens the door and shoves the person inside, slamming the door shut. The murderer usually grabs the bars and cries out, but the guard jingles the keys and turns away. The prisoner is left alone to sit on the bed in a tiny room, pacing the floor until the guard once again comes for him. This time, the destination is a room with a chair. The guard shoves the murderer down in the seat and straps him in tight. Then he's left alone again while the people in the outside room wait to flip the switch.

"Emmie! Are you done yet? Your Daddy is coming over to see you."

Mommy knocked on the bathroom door and told me to hurry up.

"Quit fooling around and give Janey and Cissy a bath in your water while it's still warm."

She brought them in, and I put them into the tub. They played and splashed, making me wet again. When we were done, we came out of the bathroom wrapped in towels.

"Put on your other shorts set, the one you wear for special occasions. And make Janey wear hers too."

When I heard that, I got them both dressed in a hurry. Cissy had to wear rubber pants over her diaper. I put her pink dress on her, the one with the ruffles around the neck. Her brown hair was just beginning to grow. I used my comb on her head and she laughed.

"Go wait by the door, Cissy."

Janey's blond curls were hard to comb but finally, she was ready. She looked cute with her sleeveless white top and shorts. We had to wear our same old tennis shoes, but we didn't have any more socks. I wore my lime green pedal pushers and my polka dot shirt.

Janey saw him first. She was looking out the front window and searching all the cars that drove by.

"Daddy's here! Daddy's here!"

I let him inside our apartment. He walked all around the big pole and looked in the kitchen. The first one of us he picked up was Cissy. Janey jumped up and down.

"Me too, Daddy. Pick me up."

"Oh, you are heavy, girls. Let's go for a drive."

We left Mommy there alone, drinking her coffee and polishing her white waitress shoes. The first place we went was Sablosky's Department Store on Massachusetts Avenue. The woman inside put new shoes on Cissy's feet. Our little sister never had any since she didn't walk much. Now she had a new pair of white baby shoes. The saleslady put a pair of white ruffled socks on Cissy then measured her feet on a metal board. The woman climbed up on a rolling ladder that stretched all the way up to the ceiling. We watched her slide the ladder from one stack of boxes to the next. It was like being entertained at the circus, seeing her take that ladder and roll across the wall of shoe boxes. The saleslady tied the laces on Cissy's feet and pulled her from the chair. Cissy started running! We didn't know she was so fast. She ran all the way to the men's department and grabbed a shirt from a display. Cissy pulled it over her face and ran away. Janey thought that was so funny, she slapped her hands together. Daddy brought Cissy back and sat her down.

"Can I have ruffled socks, too, Daddy?" Janey wanted to copy Cissy.

The saleslady brought a pair of socks just like Cissy's and pulled them over Janey's feet. She made Janey stand up on the same metal board and measured her feet. The shoes that Janey got were black leather with straps. After the woman fastened the buckles, Janey got out of her chair and began dancing around the store. I was next.

"I don't want ruffles on my socks, please."

The saleslady brought me a pair of stretchy white socks, and I told her they were very comfortable. She asked my father what kind of shoes I needed.

"School shoes," Daddy told her.

We watched again as the woman climbed on her rolling ladder. This time she used a long black stick with hands to grab some boxes. Pair after pair, they were not the right kind.

"Those brown leather ones are fine."

The shoes were made like moccasins. The lady called them penny loafers because there was a slit in the top part where I could put a penny. I turned around sideways, then back, then around again. She checked to see whether my big toes were crowded, but I had plenty of room. My feet felt very nice.

"She has to walk to school this year," Daddy told the saleslady.

On the way to the cash register, I picked up a pack of diaper pins.

"Cissy needs these, Daddy."

He took the pins and grabbed up a can of baby powder and a baby comb. The man ringing up our sale asked Daddy if we needed anything else.

"We might be back next week."

The saleslady had put our old shoes in the boxes, so we wore our new shoes out the door. Cissy didn't have to be carried anymore. We had to catch her when she ran away again. Then Daddy drove us all to the drugstore on the corner for lunch. We each sat on a stool and gave the cook our orders.

"I want a cheeseburger with pickles!" Janey said.

"Me too! And a chocolate malt" I ordered.

"Give them fries and an egg for the baby. I want the corned beef on rye."

Daddy placed our order, and we settled back to wait. There were metal boxes on the counter with lists of songs. You put in a dime to select three titles. Janey picked the first one, Pretty Woman, by Roy Orbison. She kicked her new shoes until the song was over.

"What do you want to hear, Daddy?" I asked him.

He pushed a button and a polka song started to play. He stood up and danced with Cissy in his arms like she was a big woman. Cissy was bouncing up and down in Daddy's arms until the song was over. I played a new song by the Beatles, She Loves You. I sang Yeah! Yeah! Yeah! just like they did on the record, not caring if anyone stared. We were by the magazine rack when I spotted a Beatles songbook with pictures, and Daddy said that I could buy it.

The cook had our lunch ready. Daddy fed Cissy her egg and toast between bites of his own food. Janey ate her pickles first and asked for more. She ate every bite of her cheeseburger. Daddy reached over and took some of my fries while I read my Beatles book. After lunch, Daddy bought Janey and me a roll of Lifesavers, butter rum and wintergreen for Janey.

"Don't give any to Cissy. She'll choke," Daddy warned us.

We went for a walk all around the neighborhood and Downtown. Daddy posed us on the steps of the World War Memorial and took our picture. My favorite was when I posed at the front door of the Central Library. Janey and Cissy sat by the fountains on the Circle. It was so hard to get them to sit still, I had to bribe them. I gave Janey my colored pencils. I put my rope bracelet on Cissy's arm.

"Could we go up to the top, Daddy?"

I wanted to climb up the stairs to the top of the monument. Daddy paid the guard a dime for each of us. Cissy was free. It was so hot and humid, the middle of August, but we climbed all the way to the top. The people coming down stopped to let us pass. We did not stop until we got up there. The whole city was visible. Janey stood on a metal step to see better.

"Look, there's our house and the museum," I said.

"Where is the house we used to live in?" Janey asked Daddy.

He pointed to the east then made us look south.

"There's an airplane. It's landing now."

"We're up high like an airplane, aren't we Daddy?" Janey kept pulling Daddy's arm.

Cissy pressed her face to the glass and pointed to pigeons. I looked at Daddy and saw him whispering in Cissy's ear. Janey had her hand in Daddy's, and I felt like I didn't want to go back to our apartment. But it became too hot up there, and we were sweating. Down we went, pushing ourselves against the walls as new people climbed up the monument. Outside, water from the buffalo's mouth splashed on our faces and landed in the fountains. We threw pennies in the pool and made wishes when they landed on the bottom. As we walked away from the monument, Janey asked Daddy a question.

"What is that lady's name?"

She is the one on top of the monument with her arm raised toward heaven and a sword in the other. She looked like an angel.

"Her name is Lady Victory," Daddy answered, and we stared up some more.

On the way home, I walked backward eating my Lifesavers. I wanted to see the lady for as long as possible. We walked all the way up Meridian Street, and I could see her until we turned the corner on 16th Street. I peeked back one more time, and she was still guarding the whole city as we walked back home. Daddy took us back to our apartment. Mommy was busy ironing her waitress dress when we came in.

"My girls are home."

Daddy walked over to her and put some money on the kitchen table.

"Here. Buy the girls some groceries."

Mommy took the money and asked when he was coming over again.

"Next Saturday. I'll be here in the morning."

So Daddy took Janey, Cissy, and me out on a date every week from then on.

Six

Honky Tonk Woman

~⚬⚬⚬~

Mommy's friend Alice began to come over every day. I didn't like her at all. Her hair was black and ratted, and she twisted it up into a beehive. There was so much hairspray on it that her hair didn't move. I thought she looked like a clown with all that bright green eye shadow. It covered her entire eyelids up to the brows. The rest of her makeup was even worse-white lipstick and purple rouge. Alice walked into our apartment one day wearing tight white slacks that barely covered her ankles. She had on white high heels with holes cut out for her toes, and they were polished in red. Her red sleeveless blouse had sequins all over it. I watched as she paraded around our living room, dangling her earrings as she bobbed her head back and forth. They sparkled like diamonds, but she said they were fake. The perfume that she had on smelled like cinnamon and roses, and it made me cough when she stood in front of me.

"I'm gonna get me a heap of tips tonight!"

She sat at our kitchen table and crossed her legs. She took out a manicure kit from her purse. She had the longest fingernails I'd ever seen on anybody. Alice asked me for a bowl of soapy water to soak her nails to soften them. I took a mixing bowl from the cabinet and made up a bunch of suds before I sat down to watch. Each tool had a purpose. She sanded and scraped, then filed each long nail. When she painted her nails with that frosted white polish, I was amazed. Mommy my used clear polish on her nails. She did not look anything like the woman sitting at our table. Alice was so colorful and entertaining; it was like looking at the pages of a magazine. Alice never kept quiet. She smoked long skinny cigarettes that smelled of mint. I had to empty our only ashtray every few minutes, or it would overflow. She and Mommy drank two pots of coffee. Really, Alice drank the most, but Mommy never told her to leave. That woman came over every day before she and Mommy went to work. She kept trying to put lots of makeup on Mommy, but Janey and I would cry.

"Don't wear that blue eye shadow. Oh no! You look sick!"

I wondered why Alice didn't just wear a waitress uniform like Mommy did. Still, every day she came over in a different outfit. I stared at the one with black satin pants and a long-sleeved blouse or a silver dress with rhinestones and silver boots with fishnet hose. One day Alice had on the tightest pink satin pants that we'd ever seen. Her white blouse was see-through, and she had on a matching pink bra. The blouse was so tight that I thought she couldn't breathe. The ruffles on her sleeves shook as she moved. Alice walked past me, and I saw that she wore a gold belt to match her high-heeled sandals. That day, she had on gold lipstick and matching eye shadow. Alice was wobbling and leaning on the furniture. When she sat down at the table, she took out a pint of vodka from her gold bag.

"Bring me a glass, baby. Got to have me a little drink before I go to work. Where's your mother now? I told her I'd be here."

I found her a glass in the sink. It was one that Janey drank chocolate milk from for lunch. I didn't really wash it very clean, just swirled it around. I rinsed it for a few seconds and gave it to her wet. I did not feel like trying to please her.

"Got any orange juice?"

We were out, so Alice drank the vodka with lemonade. I hated her then, but I could not stop looking at her gold bracelets and rings. That day, Mommy started drinking vodka with Alice instead of coffee as they used to. One evening, Mommy forgot to make our supper before she left for work. I ran after them as they started down the stairs.

"What can we eat tonight Mommy? You didn't cook anything."

They both stopped, and Alice put both hands on the wooden railing so she would not fall down. Mommy's breath smelled bad like a bottle of alcohol. Janey was gagging from the smoke in the air.

"I don't know, Emmie. You'll have to open up some cans. Now I have to leave."

Janey and I ate chicken broth and toast with sugar. There was a can of green beans in the cabinet, but I wasn't in the mood to cook them. I gave Cissy some Jell-O water, and she went to sleep. When Daddy came on Saturdays, we had extra food. We were always hungry on the days that Mommy went to work with Alice.

Seven

Goodnight, Sweetheart, Goodnight

M ommy was too late with the rent, so Mr. Ogre kicked us out. We found an apartment on top of the tavern where Mommy worked, and we moved in. On Thursday nights, it was Band Night. We sat out in the hallway and listened to the music while Mommy and Alice served drinks for tips. Mr. Mulligan, the owner of the bar, always gave my sisters and me paper plates with cheese and sausages and crackers from the glass jars. He let me come inside for a few minutes to carry the plates out into the hallway. We had folding chairs out there and a small bench for a table. He gave us drinks in the bar glasses with balls of ice. Janey always chose pink lemonade with an olive, and I had a ginger ale with a slice of lime. Cissy had orange juice in her baby bottle. On Fridays, he cooked pizzas in the kitchen out back. I loved Friday nights. When we were finished eating, Mr. Mulligan opened the candy machine and let us choose whatever we wanted. He let us go up to the band and request one song each. There was a guitar player named Sonny Miller who played our favorites. Janey wanted to hear a cowboy song, and I would always ask to hear *"If the Good Lord's Willin' and the Creek Don't Rise."*

Then we would run back out into the hall because Mommy said that the "XIs" would get us. Since I thought that the police were after me anyway, I was scared. I always tried my best to keep my sisters out of the bar, but it was hard. When we heard our favorite songs, we danced together out in the hallway. There was a lamp on the wall above our heads, and it made just enough light to dance by. The blue light from the tavern shined out to all three of us. Cissy stood in the door and waved at Mommy as she worked. It thrilled Janey and me to hear Sonny say our names over the microphone.

"Emmie and Janey and Cissy-It's time to say goodnight."

Then he would sing a song about bedtime. We waved goodbye to everyone and went up the stairs. You could hear the band play all night long. It was loud, but we went to sleep hearing the music.

Eight

If God Will Send His Angels

❦

A boy named Johnny asked me every day to date him. I would see him when I was out walking in the neighborhood. I knew that I was too young, so I always said no. His sister Vernice came to our apartment and asked if I could go to the movies with her and Johnny. Mommy was dusting the television set and the coffee table. I stood and watched her as she worked that morning. We had gotten up early, and since Mommy didn't work too late the night before, she was in a housecleaning mood.

"If she goes with you, I guess you can. That Johnny's fifteen and he's too old for you."

I ran to meet Vernice and Johnny at the drugstore. I didn't like him much, but he kept pestering me. His neck was fat, and his flat-top haircut made him look older than he really was. I knew that he had just turned fifteen because I saw the birthday party going on when I passed his house the week before. Johnny's father waved to me from the porch and invited me to join them.

"Hey, wanna have a piece of cake, young lady? Your friend Johnny is fifteen today."

I noticed all the beer bottles lined up on the porch rail. It seemed that there were too many men friends of Johnny's dad and not very many kids. The chocolate cake sat on the porch ledge. I was hungry, and I was tempted to go up on the porch. Then I heard one of the men say something that sounded as if it had a double meaning, and I was a little afraid of him. The other men laughed and patted Johnny on the back. I kept going and shouted out that I had to babysit for my sisters. All the men laughed again real loud.

Vernice was paying for the movie that day. We were going to see *El Cid* at the Indiana Theater downtown. She was waiting on the corner of 16th and Pennsylvania, and then the three of us walked over to the bus stop on Meridian Street. I was the first to get on the bus when it came to a stop. But Johnny tricked me. He got on the bus next and left Vernice behind. As the bus sped away, I saw her back there smiling.

"Why isn't Vernice the bus?"

"Because I wanted to get you alone."

He had such a sneaky look on his face. I didn't like the way he smiled at me. For the whole ride, I sat far away from Johnny. I pressed my body as far as I could on the side of the bus, and he scooted in next to me. He sat there with a big grin on his face and his head far back. The fat from his neck hung over his shirt collar, and I stared the whole time down at his hairy right hand. It rested on top of his knee, and I prayed that it would stay there. Johnny paid our admission at the theater, and we went inside. He bought me a box of popcorn and a cherry coke. I placed my snacks on the seat next to me so that Johnny couldn't touch me. Two huge people, a man and a woman, sat on the other side of Johnny, crushing him. I had plenty of room in my seat near the wall. Once, I looked over at him, and he winked at me. All I wanted to do was just see how he was acting, but he must have thought that I was flirting. He winked at me, and his green eyes seemed to glow in the dark at me like a big cat. Johnny leaned over and put his right arm over the back of the seat between us. He began leaning farther and farther toward me. I kept eating my popcorn and staring at the movie. Once, Johnny's hand touched my shoulder, and I yelled at him.

"I'm not going to kiss you!" I gave him my most glaring look.

"Be quiet! Shut up kid," the couple yelled at me.

People all around were speaking loudly to me. Johnny grunted and moved back into his own chair. He ate an entire box of Milk Duds and a bag of Chocolate Malted Milk Balls. It seemed like he was mad all during the movie, but I didn't care.

It was late afternoon when the show was over. Johnny spent all his money on candy and drinks, so he didn't have the fare for the bus. We walked home all the way up Meridian Street. One time, he tried to hold my hand, but I didn't let him. When we got to the tavern, I left him outside. I slammed the outer door that led to the apartments upstairs and went to find Mommy. I never did tell her that I had a date with Johnny. She thought that Vernice was with us.

"Mommy, I'm home now."

She patted me on the arm and smiled at me.

"I got paid today. We're having catfish tonight."

Mommy and I cut up the fish into small pieces and rolled them in flour and cornmeal. She told me to sprinkle them with salt, pepper, and paprika.She melted a big scoop of lard in her black iron skillet, and I watched as she dropped the fish into the hot grease. It bubbled and popped out at me.

"Cut up some tomatoes and onions. We're having a salad with Thousand Island dressing. When you're finished with that, you make macaroni and cheese."

Mommy also made corn cakes with butter and honey. Janey said it was the best supper she'd ever had.

"Honey, you say that every time I cook."

Mommy didn't drink any vodka that day. When supper was over, we took our kitchen chairs and sat downstairs on the sidewalk. Cissy played on the stairs with a miniature truck and kept throwing it down to Janey. I sat next to Mommy, and we watched people. She didn't have to work at the tavern, and I didn't have to babysit. All the people who walked by said that we were very nice girls.

One night when I was babysitting, I read my Nancy Drew Mystery *The Hidden Staircase*. Daddy had given it to me when he found out that I was interested in detectives. Nancy was visiting some people who lived in an old house. They were out in the country, and a storm began to brew. Outside my window, the wind began to blow just like in the story. Nancy woke up to investigate. She threw on her flannel wrapper and lit an oil lamp by her bed.

I came to the part in the book where Nancy started downstairs, and then I heard something squeaking outside in my hallway. The floorboards snapped and moved whenever someone walked on them. I could see the feet beneath the door. I closed my book and watched as the light outside in the hall came under the space of the door into the dark apartment. When I heard someone coming, I had turned off the lamp. I knew that it was not Mommy or Alice because they rattled their keys when they came up. I couldn't see anyone out the peephole, but I heard breathing out there. I held my breath. My stomach got tight. It felt as if something big and scary was inside of me, and I had to force it out. Then someone put something in the keyhole. The knob was turning, going round and round. But I was so scared that I just stood there until the person came in. It was Johnny, and his green eyes were shiny in the dark. His neck bulged over the collar of his plaid shirt. I hadn't noticed until then how big his teeth were or how tall he was.

"Emmie!"

He came toward me with a screwdriver in his hand. There was a bad smell coming out of him like chemicals at the hardware store. Sweat dripped down his cheeks, and his shirt was wet under the arms. There were stains on his jeans and something black smeared all over his skin. When he came toward me, he began to pant and roar. A face of a tiger covered his own face, and his fingers turned into claws. Johnny's shirt faded away, and his chest was covered with hair. The smell turned stronger, and his breath was coming out like fire.

"You're not supposed to be here Johnny. Mommy said that you're too old for me!"

His right arm reaches out to grab me, but I step back. I am falling backward over the coffee table. I am lying there on the floor, watching the screwdriver coming down at me.

"Then no one will get your pretty face."

The animal roars, springs over the table, and pounces toward me. Then I begin to go away somewhere.

I smile at the guard,and he points to a room of new paintings. But the beast tears my shirt, and I can hear the cloth ripping. I sit on a cool stone bench to admire my favorite painting, The Prodigal Son Returns. How loving the father is, I think. There he is with outstretched hands come to meet his child. The colors of the fabric are rich that he gives his son, wrapping him up in a cape. He hands him jewels and fresh fruit and bread on a platter. Servants stand all around to help him home. There is soft music playing, a flute and a harp drift over toward me. The guard folds his arms across his chest and taps the keys in his pocket. It is night, and the museum is about to close.

Johnny has the screwdriver pressing into the side of my neck.
   "You won't let me kiss you, you little bitch. You tease. I'll do it my way!"

The Prodigal Son wears dirty, torn clothing. He doesn't even have any shoes on his feet. Yet all his brothers and family come to greet him. They bring pitchers of water to clean his face and hands.

My knees are tight, closed against invasion. The beast tries hard with his hands to open them, but I am locked. He can't get inside. The chemicals are suffocating me, and the smell of his sweat chokes my lungs.

I dream of smells at the Father's house. It is rich with flowers, perfume, and oils. The sisters all bring platters of meat and fish to the hungry traveler. I reach out for the food as it comes near.

I am moaning and crying, holding closed so that he can't get in. The weapon presses down into my face, pushing but not breaking my skin. I see Janey. She has the broom, and she knows what to do. She's screaming and beating Johnny on the back, yelling "Mommy, Mommy, Mommy, Mommy!" Then Alice comes into the room.
   "You bastard punk, you! Get OFF her. I'll tear your eyes out with my ten

fingers and stuff 'em down your throat. Get! Now!"

Alice starts squeezing Johnny's neck with her hands. The silver polish sparkles on her nails as she presses harder and harder. He rises up like a giant animal, smashing her down on her back. The sound that comes out of him is like the voice of a demon. It screams and groans and roars as it slinks back out into the hallway.

The guard lets me out of the museum. "We're closing, daughter. You're always welcome to visit us." I will go back the next day and see the father stretch out his hands.

My arms are upraised, and blood is dripping down them. I have pierced my fingers into his back. They are warm and covered with something greasy and black, the same thing smeared all over Johnny's skin. Alice bends down and how lovely is her creamy white gown. Her long black hair flows down her shoulders, and she smells like Ivory soap.

"I didn't have to work. I was inside my apartment resting when I heard a little kitten. But I couldn't find him anywhere. Your door was open, and I saw Janey holding the broom."

We looked out the front window and spotted Johnny running down the street away from the building before the police arrived. Mommy came upstairs and stood in the corner whispering to the policeman. I overheard some of the things he said.

"We can't be sure of her injuries. Watch her and see if she gets any disease. You could go to the emergency room, but they wouldn't treat her very nice. People tend to blame the victim. They would just send you home and tell you to give her aspirin. The best thing is to give her a bath in warm water. Her attacker was probably high on glue and bennies. There've been several of these assaults this year."

After the police left, I told Mommy I was hungry. She drove us to the White Castle by the Central Library. I ate six hamburgers, fries, and two large orange drinks. Some people stared at us funny. My face was cut. Alice still had on her long white nightgown. Mommy had on her work uniform. I held Cissy on my lap. She was wearing a tee shirt and a diaper. Janey wore her favorite shorty gown and her new shoes. I'd wrapped a blanket around my shoulders because I was so cold. We sat at the counter for two hours, Mommy and Alice drinking drinking coffee.

"Tomorrow, we're moving," Mommy told us.

Alice bought us a lemon pie to eat in the car. A little striped kitten was meowing by our door. I picked him up. We locked the door. Mommy stayed awake all night. Our radio played a program from Chicago, *Blues for the Night.* Tiger, my new kitten, crawled in bed with Teddy and my sisters and me that night.

Nine

Shiny Happy People

❧

We moved to our apartment over on Alabama Street, a few blocks away just in time for school. My new teacher, Mr. Ramsey, at Indianapolis Public School Number 45, was very friendly. He was a black man and the first male teacher that I had ever had. All my other teachers had been nuns at Saint Phillip Neri, Saint Bernadette, Saint Simon and Holy Spirit School. I would be in a public school, and I did not have to wear a uniform. I quickly found out it was a different type of school, too easy for me. I knew all the answers. After a few days, Mr. Ramsey asked me to let the other kids answer his questions. I think he tried extra hard one day in geography to trick me. I had to borrow the World Atlas from the library to find the answers. The students did not write much at public school. The sisters required us to use fountain pens with our own ink cartridges. Every day at my Catholic school, the children wrote an essay answering a question on the board. I raised my hand.

"Mr. Ramsey, when are we going to write?"

"Write?" He looked at me puzzled.

"You'll write when you take a test."

For our first quiz, he handed out yellow pencils. I had not used a pencil since first grade except for math or art classes. I answered all the questions in five minutes. I was the first person to hand Mr. Ramsey their paper. I sat at my desk and watched the clock. If they didn't finish soon, we'd have to leave for lunch.

"Emmie, go to the office and turn this box of pencils back in."

Mr. Ramsey was smiling. He had big shoulders and a wide grin. He wasn't old, but he wasn't young, and his hands always seemed so smooth. I guess I didn't need to learn whatever he taught the other students while I was gone. The secretary made me wait in a line with the other students who were turning in pencils also. I had to sign my name and the time on a list of borrowed supplies. It took about 10 minutes, and it was time to leave for lunch when I returned to class. After that day, I began to hand in reports to Mr. Ramsey such as "The Birds of North America" or "Limestone-Indiana's Gift to the World." He liked my reports.

"I guess I'll have to give you extra credit in the appropriate subject even though you already have excellent grades."

When I wrote reports on the artists of some of my favorite paintings, Mr. Ramsey called me up to his desk.

"Where did you learn about Monet and Renoir? How did you research Van Gogh?"

"At the museum. I go there almost every day."

He especially liked my report on sculptors. I described a statue of the Virgin Mary holding the body of Jesus on her lap after he died on the cross. The name was La Pieta or The Pity. This statue was not in our museum, but I had seen the picture in an encyclopedia. I also wrote a biography of Michelangelo.

"You have 100 in art, Emmie."

My paper had gold and blue stars at the top and a big red check mark next to my name.

Mr. Ramsey shook my hand and started writing something in his grade book. We had to go to a lot of meetings in public school. The nuns at my other schools used to make us kids stand up in front of the class and read catechism and history books. Or we discussed theology and philosophy for hours. Nobody had time to go to any meetings. At public school, the students had to go to meetings two or three times a week. We listened to people tell us how to bathe and use the right deodorant. Sometimes, a policeman or fireman would give safety talks. The nurse talked about good health, and we lined up for hearing tests, eye tests and tests on our spine. We were measured and photographed, and dentists examined our teeth. One day, a nurse squirted a gooey liquid on our heads that smelled like the oil Mommy always used on her sewing machine. This liquid was supposed to kill lice. A group of women in long white coats came one day and asked all the students to place their sweaters and jackets in a large box in the hallway. Mr. Ramsey shut the door, but the odor came in any way. Some of the girls started coughing, and one boy gagged and spit on the floor. It was bug spray. I knew because I heard the words fumigation and eradication. After school, we took our clothes out of the box. I would not wear my sweater on the way home.

Gym class was strange also. We had to buy a pair of shorts and a big white shirt from the school. The shirt looked like a doctor's shirt. Everybody looked alike, and all our shirts were too big. Mommy almost didn't have enough money, but Daddy gave me the rest. I hated to change my clothes in front of the other girls. Outside, the gym teacher made us do stupid exercises with our arms. Up! Down! Up! Down! Bend your waist! Clap your hands! I kept thinking how silly we all looked. Why don't we just play kickball like in Catholic school? Or we could play tag. The students never needed to change their clothes, and it was called recess, not gym class. We had to kick the ball and run, and it was a lot more fun than jumping around like monkeys. Sister Felicia would blow her whistle, and we'd line up all out of breath. Now there I was, wearing a stupid shirt that made me feel like an old man, making me so angry. And it seemed like we were in some kind of place like the Army, but we were too young.

After lunch one day, Mr. Ramsey introduced me to George. He was a new student from China.

"Since you are so smart, Emmie, I am going to let you help George. You can tell him what he needs to know. Plus, he lives close to you."

George sat next to me, and I pointed to the pages in his book. I showed him the right book to use and even turned the page since he didn't know the numbers in English. I walked him home after school.

"What's your last name, George?"

He looked at me with those big black eyes.

"George, what is your last name?"

He still stared at me, so I took a piece of paper and wrote my name "Emmie O'Brien."

"Look! Emmie is my first name and O'Brien is my last name. Now, what is yours?"

I pointed to myself and then pointed to the name on the paper. I did this back and forth a few times. Then George's eyes opened up even bigger, and he seemed to understand me. We had our history books with us, and he turned to the page where there was a story of the first president of the United States.

"George Washington? You're from China! Well, I guess you can be named George Washington if you want to."

George's grandmother was waiting on the front steps for him. She was tiny and wore sandals even though it was the first of October. I thought I could fit into her shirt, but her short black pants looked funny. She bowed her waist to me and said something in Chinese.

"Yo yo yo yo yo yo"

I think she said to come and get George in the morning, but I wasn't sure.

"Bye George! Bye Grandma!"

Janey was with us, and I led her home. One Sunday, I saw George and his grandma walking down Alabama Street carrying a metal bucket and a cloth bag. They stopped in front of my house and waved to me on the front steps. George's grandma said something to me in Chinese.

"What did she say, George?"

He stuttered, "You go. We go to water."

George couldn't speak English very well, but he was learning a few words. When he pointed to the bucket, I understood. They wanted to do something by the water-maybe collect rocks or leaves. Mommy said that I could go with them to Fall Creek. It was the only water anywhere near our neighborhood. We walked all the way to Fall Creek Boulevard near Central and Meridian. We climbed down the banks to the water. The sun was shining, and it was warm for October. Grandma sat the bucket down and spread out her sweater for a tablecloth. We ate egg rolls with pieces of fish and mushrooms. George poured me a cup of warm tea from a glass jar. It was green tea, a little bitter but sweet at the same time. Together, we watched the water flowing in front of us. Squirrels gathered acorns from the ground around us and ran back up the trees. A family of crows nested under the bridge, the father crow trying to catch some of the carp that swam in the creek. A turtle slowly crossed a log from one side of the bank to the other. Downstream, two old fishermen cast their poles out into the water. Two blue herons sat on a stump and looked all around.

Grandma fell asleep with her arm across her eyes. She had rolled up her sweater into a pillow and turned over on her side. George and I began to hunt for money. We found two dimes and a gold bracelet. I put the bracelet on my arm. George picked up a black rock that was shaped like an egg. It was smooth and shiny. We searched the creek banks, but we couldn't find any more.

When Grandma woke up, she joined us. She took off her sandals so she could stand up in the water. Her pants were rolled up above her knees. She laughed and looked very young then. We did what she did. When Grandma reached down and scooped up a little crawdad with her hands, we scooped one up also. The three of us piled them in the bucket until it was full. They kept trying to crawl out of our fingers, but we dumped them fast into the bucket. Grandma poured water on top of them. Then she placed her sweater on top.

We walked all the way home with that heavy bucket, stopping to rest now and then. George invited me into their house when we got to the door. They had birds in cages in all the rooms-blue birds, yellow birds, white birds and a singing green bird with feathers sticking straight up out of his head. One of the birds got loose and flew over to me. It flew around my head and landed on my shoulder. He was talking and poking at my head with his beak.

George took the bird and put it in his hands. I had never seen anyone own birds as pets. And the birds understood Chinese.

Grandma told us to come into the kitchen. She washed the crawdads and dumped them all into a big kettle of boiling water. I watched as she opened all her little jars of spices and added a pinch of each to the pot. With a long-handled spoon, she stirred the crawdads. Steam was getting thick in the room. She chopped something green and added it to the kettle. When she dropped turnips into the liquid, I turned to George.

"What is it?"

"Soup. Eat Soup."

I was scared then. Not of George or Grandma, I was scared of the crawdads. I knew how crunchy they sounded when they landed in the bucket, and how their pincers caught hold of your skin. My mother never cooked soup with crawdads. I began to look at the door. Then George's parents walked in. I had never met them. George's father spoke English very well.

"We have a guest in our home. Please join us for a meal."

George's mother bowed to me just like Grandma. All four of them smiled at me, so I said okay. They gave me some vegetables and sauce, cold like a salad. The noodles were delicious. But when Grandma placed the bowl of soup in front of me, I was glad it only had one crawdad. I ate the turnip first, and then the green leaves. I sipped most of the broth. That crawdad kept looking up at me with his tiny eyes. That's when George's father smiled at me.

"Dear guest, you appear to be finished."

Then he spoke Chinese very fast to Grandma. She removed my bowl with the crawdad away from me. I sat there while they all crunched their crawdads and sipped broth from the bowl. Everyone turned their bowls up and drank it without their spoons. George's father even asked for another bowl of soup with extra crawdads. I was happy when Grandma served dessert-dried fruit in a bowl. I picked mine up like the rest of the family did with their hands. The pineapple was the best. It was almost dark, and Mommy would be worried about me. She asked me what I ate at George's house.

"Crawdad soup and turnips."

"Oh, Emmie. You're always meeting the strangest people!"

Mommy hugged me and said she missed me all day long. She was drinking coffee and writing letters to all her relatives in Tennessee. I would buy her some stamps after school the next day and go mail them for her.

"George's grandma taught me how she caught crawdads."

I knew I would never cook them in soup. I went to sleep seeing those eyes staring up at me, their little black bodies floating around in the kettle.

Ten

Follow the Yellow Brick Road

❦

I had been watching the gypsies for a few weeks. They always sat outside their candy store on 22nd Street. On my way home from school one afternoon, a woman spoke to us.

"You like to buy some candy, little children?"

Janey and George said nothing, but I said okay. The woman stuck out her hand to me and touched me. I wasn't afraid. Her arm had six gold bracelets, all a different design. While she led me, I studied her. She was middle-aged, medium height, and her skin was soft and rosy like a young girl. Her hair was black, and it fell all the way down her back to her knees. When she moved, her hair moved also. She wore a long black skirt, very full and a blouse of many colors. Her eyes were dark brown and so were her heavy brows. Her face did not have any makeup on it, yet she appeared to be painted. When she smiled at me, her pink lips opened wide.

"Here. You like lemon? You like cherry or oranges? Perhaps you like vanilla?"

She stuck a sour lemon ball in my mouth. It was covered with sugar, but after I had it in my mouth for a few seconds, the coating melted. The taste of lemon was so strong, so wonderful. Janey stared at the gypsy woman, so she put a piece of root beer candy in my little sister's mouth. George had hot cinnamon candy. The three of us stood there rolling the candies around in our mouths and trying to suck all the flavor out.

"Three cents! You like candy now?"

I paid for our candy with one of the dimes I found that day with George and Grandma. We walked around the gypsy store. They had jewelry for sale and women's stockings displayed on plastic legs. There were foam heads with scarves tied around them—just heads with no faces as if they were out walking in the wind. A few of the heads had on sunglasses like movie stars. A row of hands on a shelf wore gloves of every color. I spotted a pair of long black velvet ones, and I wanted them. There were hats for men and women. My favorite was a green felt hat with a small veil.

"Want to wear the hat girl?" the gypsy lady asked.

She took the hat from the faceless model and placed it on my head, arranging the veil until my eyes were covered. I could see Janey and George staring at me as if I were somebody else.

"Look in the mirror, little lady. Green is your color!"

She spun me around by the shoulders until I felt dizzy. I looked at myself in the scratched mirror she held in front of me. Where could I wear the hat—to the museum, to school or when I walked to the meat market?

"Six dollars. You got a name, little girl? I am Bernadette."

"I'm Emmie."

"Emmie, you pay me six dollars, I give you the hat. Yes?"

I told her that I only had one more dime.

"Okay. Come back when you have six dollars."

Janey and George and I left the store, and we felt disappointed. The gypsy woman had such tasty candy and all those hats to play with. We said that we'd go back when we had more money. The next morning, Bernadette was waiting when we passed by.

"Hey, Emmie. I got something for you."

She wiggled her finger at me to come closer. A little girl came out of the building. Her skin was dark and rosy, and her black hair stretched down to her waist just like the gypsy woman.

"This is Polly, my daughter."

I looked at the girl with the gold bracelets and dangling earrings.

"Hi Polly!"

I couldn't think of anything else to say to her. I just kept on staring at her long skirt with all the colors. It looked like she was wearing a rainbow around the bottom half of her body. Her white blouse seemed like it was brand new. Around her waist, she had on a black velvet belt that tied in a bow.

"You take Polly to school," Bernadette ordered me.

I finally found words to speak. "What grade is she in?"

"Your grade!"

All I could do was let Polly go with me when her mother pushed her toward me. Polly walked behind George all the way. Mr. Ramsey stood up and came to the door. We were right in time for the bell.

"Who is this, Emmie?"

"It's Polly. She is in this grade, and I brought her to school. She just moved here from Romania."

My teacher took Polly and found her a desk on the other side of me. He moved another girl over to the window seat. Now I had two people who needed help, George and Polly. She never said anything, but every day when I said I liked her skirt or her hair ribbons, she smiled at me. Her mother gave me a paper bag of candy after the first week.

"Polly is learning many new things. You want to meet her sisters?"

I followed the gypsy into the back of her store through the shiny gold curtains. When we entered the kitchen, there were ten women all the same as Polly, only older.

"This is Margaret, Megan, Shannon, and Casey. Here is Kelly, Erin, Bridget, Peggy, Mary, and Frances in the back row."

They all had Irish names, just like the girls at St. Simon's. Instead of redheads and blonds and light brown hair, these women had shiny black hair and dark eyes. Each one wore a skirt like Polly's.

"When we came to America, we chose American names."

Then Bernadette brought each of the women to me. I said hello, and each one nodded and smiled.

"They don't speak your language yet. I am the only one. I came here first. My husband, their father, is coming when he is set free from the prison. He isn't bad. He was taken because we are gypsies. When something happens, the people think it is us. We are different."

Bernadette then showed me what the women had been working on before I came in. There were bowls of flowers and seeds along with jars of oil. Each woman had a certain job. One ground the seeds with a stone on a flat board; another whipped the oil into foam with a wooden spoon. I saw one of them tearing flowers into tiny pieces and another sister crushing the petals with a rolling pin on the counter top. At the end of the line, several women blended the mixture in a wooden churn, like butter is made on the farm.

"Are you making fresh butter?" I asked.

"No. We make cream for beautiful faces."

The last two sisters spooned the yellow mixture into small glass jars and glued labels on them. I read the words Romanian Dreams Beauty Cream.

"I write the words, and then we sell the cream," Bernadette told me.

The sisters were giggling. One of them came and lifted up my braid and examined it. She bent down and looked into my eyes. She studied my face and my hands. Then she told her sisters something in her language. All of them giggled again real loud.

"They say that you will not have trouble finding a husband and that your skin does not need beauty cream. They ask what you put on your skin."

"I don't use anything, only soap."

"You tell everyone you use our cream. They believe you. We will be rich, okay?"

They all giggled again and said things I didn't understand. Bernadette pointed to the dining room table.

"You like pork soup?"

I didn't know what she was talking about, but I was hungry. One of the women set a bowl of soup in front of me and waited while I tasted it. There were chunks of meat and cabbage, with some of the same seeds that they used for the beauty cream. I ate all of it. They filled my bowl again, and I finished that. The sisters kept stirring, crushing, and packing, smiling at me all the while.

"You take this to your mother."

It was a big glass jar of soup, still hot. Bernadette led me through the store out to the sidewalk. She pinched my cheek and made the sign of the cross over me.

"You come back tomorrow. I want you to sell Romanian Dreams Beauty Cream."

So that's how I began my after-school job as a sales girl. Everywhere that I went, I had a small box of face creams. I sold them for a dollar, and my profit for each was a dime.

Polly started to go with me to the bowling alley after school. She liked the sound of the ball knocking over the pins. Every time someone made a strike, she clapped her hands, and all her bracelets made a clinking sound. We sat by each group as they rolled their balls down the aisles. When no one was playing, Polly and I tried to lift the heavy bowling balls. We tried every one of them, but they were all too big. Polly liked to spin the colored balls around on the floor since we didn't have any money to play. We sat on the leather benches watching the groups of players jump up and down. They hit each other on the back and whistled when they did something right.

Our favorite group was The Methodist Hospital Retired Nurses' League. The ladies all wore matching pink blouses with their names stitched above their pockets and the name of the group in large letters across their backs. Each woman wore white slacks and white nursing shoes. We sat and watched as they took off their white shoes and changed into bowling shoes. I wanted to bowl, but I did not want to wear those ugly bowling shoes. They must have all went to the same beauty parlor because they had the same hairdo-short and curly. I made friends with Marvena. She was the most talkative one.

"Honey, if you go get me a coke, I'll buy you and your friend one too."

I took the money she handed me and hurried over to the counter. Polly tasted her first chocolate cola that day. All afternoon, we brought cigarettes and drinks to the nurses' league. At the end of their game, Marvena let Polly and me roll some balls down the aisle.

"Throw your right arm back and your right knee forward. Slowly raise up and let the ball roll away from your fingers. Just give it a little push when you take your fingers out of the holes."

Mine went in the gutter. Polly did exactly as Marvena said, and the ball knocked over all the pins. There was Polly, twirling around on the wooden floor as if she was dancing at the ball, her rainbow skirt twirling around her legs. Her bracelets made little sounds like music when they hit together. Everyone in the nurses' league clapped when she finished twirling. The women laughed and gave her the prize of the week. It was a teacup and saucer-white with Irish shamrocks in green and rimmed in old. Polly held the prize in her hands, and she wanted to say thank you. But she looked at me, mumbling and pulling on my sleeve.

"Polly says thank you! When she can speak English, she'll tell you herself. She really loves the prize of the week."

The two of us walked slowly so we wouldn't drop the cup. I stood outside in front of their house. The curtains were open, and I saw Polly holding the cup and saucer like she was going to serve tea to her family. I could see her from far away and her rainbow skirt. That day, Mommy began using the beauty cream and drinking tea out of a crystal cup from the gypsy store. It was sparkling when the light hit the cup, and the tea was golden.

"It soothes my nerves. When I get paid, I'm going to buy another cup. By next year, I will have a set of eight. I need to buy another box of their tea."

One day after school, Mommy asked me to do the laundry. I took Janey and Cissy in the wagon since it was only one block away. Cissy loved to go for a ride. All the people waved at her when we crossed the street. I dumped all our clothes into two big washers. Cissy pressed her face on the window and watched all the bubbles and suds. I loved to go to the Laundromat because they had stacks of magazines. Janey sat by me while I read Reader's Digest cover to cover. I watched what the other women did. I matched our socks and folded Cissy's diapers into squares. Janey tried to help me fold the sheets, but she kept dropping the sheet on the floor. It got all wrinkled. She was scared, but I did not yell at her. We didn't have a basket, so I turned a pillowcase inside out like another woman did. All the clothes stayed clean

50

on the way home with Cissy in the wagon.

Eleven

Stand By Me

On Halloween, I took Janey, George and Polly trick-or-treating while Mommy stayed home with the baby. All the kids in the neighborhood were out. Polly wore her everyday clothes. I helped George decorate a sheet, and he became a ghost. He understood enough English, but neither he nor Polly had ever trick- or-treated before. I didn't have a costume. I just wore a scarf on my head and drew fake freckles with Mommy's eyebrow pencil. We all carried pillowcases like the other kids to collect candy. Some people gave apples, homemade fudge, or caramel corn balls. Others gave away cookies and taffy. We stopped to sample the fudge on Mrs. O'Leary's front steps. George opened the wax paper and examined the fudge as if it was something weird. He stared at it for a few seconds, even holding it up to his nose for a smell.

"It's chocolate, George. You cook it with milk and sugar and then cut it into squares."

That's when Mrs. Santoni yelled at us. I jumped off the steps, she was so loud.

"Hey, you children! You come get my cream cookies. They have black walnuts from my sister's house in Franklin."

Mrs. Santoni was short with wide hips. She wore her black hair in two braids that she twisted into a bun. She came up to Janey and dumped a whole bowl of cookies into her pillowcase. We watched her standing in front of us as she held the empty bowl. It seemed like she was angry, but she was just serious and loud.

"You must come on Friday. We make ravioli. I am the best cook in this city, the world! You children grate the cheese. Have all the ravioli you can eat. Three o'clock!"

We promised her we'd be there. There were so many kids out that night, and it turned dark. I don't know how Polly got lost from us when we started walking again. We quit trick- or-treating to hunt for her. The leaves on the sidewalk crunched each time someone approached, but it wasn't Polly. I rang all the doorbells.

"Have you seen a little gypsy girl?"

All the people said yes, but they didn't see which way she went next. We circled the block. The bowling alley sign said OPEN. I hurried up to an old man who was sitting at the counter smoking a cigar, and we begged him to tell us if he had seen Polly.

"I haven't seen anybody! It's Halloween, you know."

I led Janey and George into the Laundromat, the drugstore, and the market. The museum was closed, and the neighborhood seemed to get larger. We wandered around everywhere. Then I heard someone crying in the dark. There between two houses, I saw Polly's skirt. The light from the moon made the colors glow. Someone was lying on top of her, and her pillowcase of candy lay beside her on the ground next to her head.

"Polly! Polly!"

I ran toward her, and the body on top of Polly rose up. In the moonlight, his face was like a mask, but it was not covered by anything. The form coming toward me was growling, shaking his fist at me again and again and screaming.

"I'll get you. I will never leave you. You're next. You get out of my WAYYY!"

He shoved me back, and I fell on Janey. George picked both of us up. We ran to Polly where she was still lying on the ground, covering her eyes with her hands. Her skirt was twisted up around her waist, so I smoothed it out. George picked leaves from Polly's hair, and Janey patted her arm. I took off my scarf and wiped Polly's face with it.

The animal in the background hovered near us, waited in the shadows behind us. The sounds of growling and grinding teeth came closer and closer, and strange sounds like the voices of people in pain made us cover our ears with our hands. The clouds parted then, and the moon shined down on us children. The beast circled all around us, and the sound of his screams made us afraid. We cried and knelt down beside Polly, begging the animal to go away. The light from the moon got larger until it made the yard we were in like daylight. He moaned and turned away then, taking the screams and the strange sounds with him. We could hear noises that sounded like people dying, but then after a while, it became quieter. I took my hands away from my ears and there was nothing, only the sound of Polly's crying.

"Here, Polly. Eat some of your candy."

She sat up and took a bite of her caramel cornball. Then I hurried and rang the doorbell of the house next door. The woman who answered was one of the women who sang at The House of the Lord Church.

"Child, what brings you here? It's way past trick-or-treat time now."

"Polly's been hurt by an animal. A real bad man. He keeps bothering all of us children."

The lady called the police, and they came right away. One of the officers went to get Polly's mother. We could hear her coming from blocks away. Her words of that other language floated in the air until they reached us. The words kept getting stronger and clearer, so we waited. It was like a flock of birds came down from the sky and swooped Polly off the ground. Her ten sisters came speaking loudly, rustling their skirts as they carried her back home. Bernadette followed raising her arms up to the sky as she went behind them. George and Janey and I came last with the pillowcases of candy. We made a procession all the way to Polly's house through the streets, the store and into her living room. There beneath a statue of the Virgin Mary, the sisters laid Polly down. One lit candles, the other cleaned her. The rest of her sisters brought flowers into the room. They filled the vases on the shelves, the tables, and the floor. Bernadette handed us a rosary.

"We must pray now. Do as I do."

The three of us knelt down and bowed our heads like Bernadette.

"Hail Mary, full of grace. The Lord is with thee..."

Polly wasn't crying anymore. She rested her head in the arms of her sisters who knelt around her, protecting her like a shield. I looked around, and I knew that the beast was still out there, that the streets were full of bad men. But inside, we were safe for now. The woman in blue up on the little altar smiled down at us all, her children.

"Holy Mary, Mother of God, pray for us now and at the hour of our death. Amen."

We left the house and took George home. Grandma patted me on the head and spoke Chinese. George still had his rosary in his hand as they closed the door.

"Mommy! Mommy! Polly was taken by a monster. Janey and I are okay. Don't worry."

Mommy wrapped her arms around both of us and squeezed us hard.

"Tomorrow, Daddy's coming over. Go to sleep."

I heard Cissy breathing in her playpen beside me. Janey put her arms around my neck, and we closed our eyes, closed out the evil things for the night.

Twelve

Tomorrow

P olly couldn't go to school with us for a few weeks after Halloween. Every day it was dark and cloudy when we walked past her house. Her mother would peek out the shop window and shake her head. "She's no good today. My girl might be better tomorrow."

It was lonely without her. Janey and I used to try to name the colors in Polly's skirt while we walked beside her.

"Burnt sienna, lemon drop yellow, aquamarine, candy apple red."

We wore the only dresses we had, our blue plaid jumpers from Catholic school. We didn't wear any jewelry like Polly. Our arms and fingers were bare. When we walked, it was quiet. Polly used to wear little boots that clicked on the sidewalk. My sister and I wore flat shoes that made no noise. George dressed in black pants and a white shirt. Grandma polished his shoes each morning before he got up. There was no color to George; pale skin, black eyes and shiny black hair. He was steady. We were comforted to see him always the same. Every morning, we ran up to his porch, and he'd come out to meet us, saying the same thing.

"Polly is better?"

"No, George, not today. Maybe tomorrow."

George would then ask how to spell the word tomorrow.

"T-O-M-O-R-R-O-W"

He'd repeat the word until it didn't sound funny, yet he'd keep asking the same question.

"When is tomorrow?"

"That's when everything will always be better. It's the very best day."

The three of us kept going without Polly. We walked ahead, always talking about tomorrow.

Thirteen

Let It Be

A new friend joined us one morning. We heard his heavy breathing before we saw him. Someone was huffing and blowing air, trying to catch up with us.

"Is this the way to school?"

"What grade are you in?"

"Sixth."

"You're in my class. We'll take you there."

Joe was a black boy with a big smile. He seemed happy to be with us, so he quit puffing his breath out. I looked over at him when we stopped at the corner. He grinned so big that I could see all of his teeth. He was big for his age, for sixth grade. Mr. Ramsey signed him in as a member of our class. But since he was so big, Joe couldn't fit in any of the desks. He had to sit in a chair with his books on his lap. Joe wasn't afraid to answer any questions. I thought he was very smart. Every morning, Joe met us at George's house, and we all walked together to school. He grinned at me the whole way to school. One day, he pulled something out of his pocket and handed it to me. It was a biscuit with ham, still warm from the oven and wrapped in a napkin.

"It's for you, Emmie."

"Thank you, Joe. Did you cook this?"

"No, my mama did. She's always cooking."

I ate a bite of the biscuit, so big and fluffy. Janey gave that look of hers when she wants something. I gave her half and offered George the rest.

"Thank you. No. I ate rice."

It was true. Sometimes, we had to wait while George finished his breakfast. We could see through the glass in the front door where his family had bowls of rice in front of them. The bowls were shiny red with gold leaves painted on the sides. His mother and father had on their American clothes. They finished their rice and said goodbye to George and Grandma, always nodding to Janey and me as they went down the steps. George said that his parents worked for the government.

"Are they mayors or governors? Do they work for the FBI? Are they policemen or how about firemen? Soldiers or spies?"

It took George a while to think about all my questions. We were walking very slowly when he blurted out his answer.

"They clean the floors."

We walked some more as he explained. "My father is a doctor. My mother is a nurse."

My mind was filled with questions.

"Then why do they clean floors for the government?"

George was very quiet.

"Yesterday-in China. Today-in U.S.A."

We were almost to our classroom when George tapped me on the shoulder.

"Tomorrow, I will be a doctor. I speak English. I study hard."

When Mr. Ramsey asked a very hard question about the human body, George's hand shot straight up in the air. I'd never seen him so lively, telling everyone about the circulatory system. He was jumping all day long in his seat, not even asking me one thing.

Joe invited us to play at his house one day. Mommy said yes, I could go if his mother was home. The lady who opened the door was the singer from the House of the Lord church, the one who called the police on Halloween. She was big like Joe. Her gray dress had little white flowers all over it, and she wore a red apron around her waist.

"Come in little children! Enter my kitchen. I've got sugar cookies for all of you."

Joe's mother had a Formica table with benches like a restaurant. We slid in and took seats all around it. She stood at the end of the table and asked us what we wanted to drink.

"Lemonade, tea, milk or cocoa?"

Every one of us ordered a different thing. The plate she sat in front of us was piled high with golden brown cookies. We each had our own place mat and a cup and saucer.

"Grab a handful. There's more on the way."

The kitchen was warm. I glanced at the oven and could see more cookies baking. Joe showed us how to dunk our cookie into our drinks, and then take a bite with our heads turned sideways. He said we could get more into our mouths that way. Janey grabbed them as fast as Joe's mama put them on the plate. I was afraid there wouldn't be enough for everybody. George, of course, wanted to know the ingredients.

"Sugar and sugar and lots of butter, honey."

Joe's mama sang as she told how she made the cookies, making sure we ate as many as we wanted.

"Could I have a refill?"

She poured me more cocoa from her metal pot. I blew the foamy part around in my cup and looked at my friends. I thought of Polly, and I knew that she would love to be eating cookies with us. Then I had an idea.

"Let's go see Polly. We'll take her some cookies if your mother says yes."

Joe's mama agreed, so we wrapped a dozen in a grocery sack. We were excited and hurried out the door.

"Thank you, Mrs. Dorster. We'll come back again."

On to way to Polly's, it turned cold and started to snow. Flakes fell lightly as we hurried to Polly's house. But then the sun came out from behind the clouds. How bright it was, the day we saw Polly. The sky was pink and blue, and the snow blew softly all around. Bernadette greeted us so joyfully when we entered the store.

"We want to see Polly. Is she better today?"

She led us through the store to the living room. Polly sat with a copy of *Little Women* on her lap.

"Hello. I am reading."

"I read that book before, Polly. It's by Louisa May Alcott, and it has a great plot. The characters are very believable. You'll like it."

Polly didn't have her skirt and blouse on that day. She wore her nightgown with a crocheted scarf around her shoulders like an old woman. She looked skinny and hungry. Joe stuck out his hand and gave her the cookies.

"I'm Joe. I'm new around here."

Polly looked up at him and his big smile as she took the cookies. Her face became pink. She began talking in half English, half Romanian.

"Tomorrow, I am better. I go to school again."

It was good to see our friend. We left Polly sitting there alone with the cookies. I was the last to leave. I could hear her unwrapping the paper sack as we left the room. I couldn't resist turning around and seeing Polly one more time. She waved at me and took a bite of cookie. The sun came into the room, and it was warm there. The statue of Mary was still on the altar keeping Polly company. Mary held out her hands to Polly and gave her blessings from her Son. I thought I saw Mary turn to hold out her hands to me also. The sunlight became brighter, and the smell of Bernadette's flowers was like a perfume. The other kids yelled for me. I had to leave. Polly was okay, and the evil only ruined her body, not her soul. Outside, the sun was shining on the others. The street was covered with a fine layer of snow. We went home to wait for the next day.

Fourteen

Living in America

＊＊＊

Our class was studying about the Pilgrims. It was close to Thanksgiving, and George was excited. Mr. Ramsey asked a question.

"Who knows why the Pilgrims came to America?"

George bounced up and down and waved his hand high.

"I know!"

"Alright, George, why did they come here and not go to another country?"

"The Pilgrims came to America because they could be free to worship God in their own way and not be under the rule of a king who told them how to believe."

I looked over at George and noticed that he was grinning. All the other students were quiet. They all turned around to look at George. Mr. Ramsey just stood there, his eyes big and his arms at his sides.

"You are exactly right, George! You'll get extra credit for such a complete answer."

All the way home, George had his history book open to the page with a picture of the first Thanksgiving dinner. He almost stumbled and fell into the street. Joe pulled him back by the collar. George talked fast, the words got jumbled, but I knew what he meant.

"I want to eat turkey!"

As we reached his house, George told us to wait. His mother came out on the porch with a twenty dollar bill in her hand. She leaned toward me and put the money in my hand.

"Please? Buy a turkey?"

We walked to the supermarket at 22nd and Central. I led the kids through the aisles to the meat department.

"These are turkeys, George."

He touched them all, rolling the turkeys over in the meat case. The one he finally chose was the biggest. It was twenty-seven pounds.

"It's a boy turkey. They're bigger," I told him.

The cashier squinted her eyes together as if she couldn't see right. It was a strange look. I took the money out of my pocket and handed it to her. Polly was amazed at the cash register when the bell rang.

"$5.95. You kids gonna carry that thing by yourselves?"

The turkey was so big that it wouldn't even fit in a bag, so Joe lifted it up on his shoulders like he was carrying a football down to the end line. Polly thought that was so funny that she laughed all the way home. George was full of questions.

"How do we cook it?"

"You roast it in the oven."

"With paper on?"

"NO! Unwrap it and take out the neck and the gizzards."

"What do we do with the gizzards?"

"Cook them and make gravy."

"What is gravy?"

"You pour it on your mashed potatoes."

"Potatoes? Mashed?"

I tried to explain everything. Joe jumped in to help me.

"George, you must eat rolls and butter with the dinner."

"Rolls?"

"And cranberry sauce."

"What are cranberries?"

George asked questions the entire way home. Grandma let us in while Joe put the turkey on the table. As we left, I remembered something important.

"Don't forget to thaw the turkey. It's frozen."

When I got home, Mommy was reading her favorite cookbook Southern Recipes. I told her about George's first Thanksgiving.

"Let them borrow my cookbook."

I ran back to his house and rang the bell. George's father opened the door.

"My mother says you can read this book and learn how to cook a turkey dinner."

He smiled at me and thanked me.

"I have never read a cookbook, but I must read it for my wife. I will give her the instructions. I am most eager to learn about gravy. George wants to eat gravy on potatoes."

I left, satisfied that George and his family would have their Thanksgiving dinner. It was almost dark when I saw Polly and her mother coming down the street. They were laughing and talking loud. Bernadette carried a large turkey in her arms like a baby. When she got closer, she spoke to me.

"We will eat turkey tomorrow for Thanksgiving dinner. I will thank God for Polly's health and for the nice city where we live."

Polly's earrings sparkled as she passed by me, and she smiled.

"Thank you, Emmie. You are a friend to me."

"You are welcome, Polly. You're my friend too. Happy Thanksgiving, everybody!"

I ran home before it got completely dark. Mommy had to be at work by 6:00 that night, and I could not be late. Janie and Cissy needed me.

Fifteen

Beautiful Day

D addy woke us up early on Thanksgiving morning. The sun was coming through the frosted glass door. I could see by his outline that he was holding something. When I opened the door to let him in, he rushed past me to the kitchen.

"This turkey is so heavy. Do you think you could cook it for me?"

"Mommy! Daddy brought us a turkey to eat!"

I yelled so loud that everyone came out of the bedroom. Mommy came into the kitchen wearing her striped housecoat and slippers.

"I guess we can use the oven if I have enough dishes. I'll need some more butter, and we don't have any cranberry sauce. Some rolls would be nice. I only have a pint of milk, and the mashed potatoes will take more than that. If you want any green salad, buy a fresh head of lettuce and some celery. The dressing will take black pepper. See if they have any cornstarch for my giblet gravy. I have enough cans of peas and corn for a vegetable dish. I better get busy now and put the turkey in the oven. I can get dressed while you take the kids to the store."

I guess Mommy decided to be friendly, because she told Daddy thanks for the turkey, and she smiled at him. Daddy took us to a little market that was open over on 38th Street. We bought the things that Mommy needed and some apples and a bag of flour for a pie. The smell of the turkey was already filling the house when we came back. Daddy carried Cissy around on his shoulders and Janey jumped on his back. He bounced them around until they were screaming that they were dizzy. We went for a walk in the neighborhood and played hide and seek.

Mommy cooked all the food in our cabinets. She opened every can of vegetable and made dumplings and cornbread dressing. I rolled out the piecrust and sliced the apples. There were enough for two big pies. Every pot in the kitchen was filled with something bubbling. Mommy even made the lime and pineapple Jell-O with cottage cheese. Daddy watched the parades on television with Janey and Cissy while I helped Mommy finish our cooking.

"Wake up Daddy!"

It was Cissy. She pushed his shoulder and patted his arm. He was asleep on the couch, the football game playing on TV with nobody watching. Cissy could say a few words, and she tried them on Daddy.

"Daddy eat supper!"

He carried her in his arms to the table. Mommy had serving dishes filled with all the things we'd cooked and carried the turkey to the table. It sat on a white ceramic tray, and it looked so brown and juicy. She'd arranged parsley and baked onions around it. I was so hungry and I was getting weak. But before we could sit down, Janey said a prayer out loud.

"Thank you for this dinner. Amen."

I don't know if she meant God or Daddy, but I was thrilled to have both of them at our Thanksgiving dinner. Mommy sat at one end of the table, and Daddy was at the other. He held Cissy on his lap, feeding her turkey with his fork. Janey and I looked from one end of the table to the other. It was warm in our apartment until Daddy had to go home. Mommy stood in the doorway and waved with us at Daddy. It became cold and dark, and Cissy started crying. We had to wrap her up in a blanket like a newborn so she'd stop crying.

"Cissy baby, Cissy baby, go to sleep, go to sleep."

Mommy wrapped up the leftovers for the next day. We had another slice of apple pie while we watched *Journey to the Center of the Earth* on television. Janey and I tried to figure out how Pat Boone could host the movie if he got so burned up down in the earth. Mommy told us that it was only a movie, and he didn't really die, so that's why he could talk during the commercials. The best movies were always on holiday nights. Mommy let us have warm milk with just a few spoons of coffee stirred in. The day was over, and we had to go to sleep. No one had argued, no one had cried.

Sixteen

Ding Dong! The Witch Is Dead!

The next day after Thanksgiving, I decided to go out selling beauty
cream. There was one jar left in my cardboard box when I spotted
the witch's house. It was the one with tall, skinny poles on the front
porch and the tower with only one window. All the other houses had wooden
siding. This one was covered in gray shingles, shaped like fish scales. Every
time we walked past that house on the way to school, Janey would cry. Even
the cats that sat in the tower window were scary.

"Do we have to walk on Park Street, Emmie? Can't we walk down Alabama?
Can we?"

She would cry and beg me to walk the other way, but George lived on Park.
Each time we went past the house, I would hold Janey's hand tight and pull
her along with me. I had never seen any people go in or out, but everyone
said that two old women lived there. Bernadette made Polly do the sign of
the cross whenever she walked in front of the house. George always showed
me his lucky rabbit's foot before we got close. Joe got the chills and began
shaking each time. We had to walk in front of the house. That was the fastest
way to school.

Nobody ever told me not to go there, so that day after Thanksgiving, I

68

walked up the steps. I stumbled a bit on a hole with rocky dirt in it. There was a chain by the doorknob with some kind of animal bone on the tip, maybe a bird's foot. I was careful not to touch the bone with my hand as I pulled the chain. I could hear chimes inside the house, and I waited until someone came. Their footsteps kept getting louder and louder on the wooden floor. They stopped. Nobody opened the door. I tapped on the glass, and that's when the heavy door creaked open. A tall, thin woman with her gray hair in a bun looked down at me.

"Would you like to buy a jar of Romanian Dreams Beauty cream? It costs one dollar."

The woman stared at me.

"Come inside. Yes, I will try a jar."

I stood in the hallway, and I could hear voices coming from the parlor. Someone seemed to be sick. They were moaning softly. The woman came back and told me to come into the parlor to get my money. She slid back the wooden door into the wall. The room was filled with people. I could barely see them since the velvet curtains were pulled shut. It was daytime, but they had the room almost dark. All the people sat around on chairs in a circle. There was a table with a candelabrum on it. White flames glowed in the dark.

I felt like leaving, but the woman told me again to enter the room. I felt as if I had to obey her even though she was a stranger, and I wanted to leave. I couldn't. My legs would not go out the door. They led me into the parlor. I felt as if my body was doing something I didn't want it to do. I stood at the opening of the circle, but I would not enter. The woman pushed me slowly down into a chair. The flames of the candles flickered, and a strange smell came toward me. It was like the smell of someone old and dying. My stomach began to jump inside me. I was trying to rise up from the chair, but I had no energy. The gray-haired woman handed me something. In the candlelight, I saw that it was a glass of blue liquid.

"I'm not thirsty."

My voice sounded far away from the room, but it was me. I was weak and could not say no. It was warm liquid, not a cold drink. It was just something that entered my mouth, and there was no taste, only the color blue.

Then I became sleepy and so hot. There was no air in the room, and I was falling down into a deep hole. It looked like a cave with rocks all around, and I was going farther and farther inside. My eyes wouldn't stay open. I reached out into the darkness and felt nothing. Each person in the room said something to me.

"You are stubborn!"

"So difficult!"

"How closed you are, little sweetie!"

"Nothing can take you away!"

"You cling to something you cannot see!"

"Your precious faith. HaHa! Where is it now to save you?"

"Remain with us. The all-knowing ones!"

I wanted to sleep, but I kept telling my eyes to stay open. My mind was talking to my body. Get up! Walk Out! Leave! My voice was screaming but only inside my head. My legs were numb, and my hands felt frozen. Each beat of my heart pounded like a drum. I could feel something on my shoulder like an animal, like when George's pet bird flew to me. This was different. Then the wings flapped with a sound like it came from far away just to land on me. It flew to the table and sat under the candle flames. What a large ugly bird it was, black and oily. Such large feathers. I tried to call out to Mommy and Daddy.

"Well, little dearie, don't you want to ask me anything? I will tell you the answer to whatever you say. Anything! Anything!"

Why did that one want me to ask her a question? Her voice was high and crackling. It entered my ears, exploded in my brain. Then I saw a picture in my mind of the lady in Bernadette's house-the altar, the white flowers and the women kneeling down. They were praying the rosary and asking Mary for help for little children in harm's way. The lady was smiling while she held Baby Jesus. He stuck out his hands just to me. I jumped out of my chair and ran fast for the door. The old woman of the house followed me.

"Come back for your money. Come back to me!"

The door came open, and down on the sidewalk, there was the gypsy woman with a bag of flowers. She threw them all over me, little white petals. She sprinkled me with water from a jar. Then she handed me a picture like the one I saw a few minutes before. It was the Virgin and Baby Jesus with his arms stretched out to me. I looked back at the witch's house. All the windows were black. Bernadette took my hand and led me down the street.

"You only sell where I tell you. Do not go back to that house again. You are fine. I can see that no one hurt you. But you are weak, and you must be strong."

When we got to my house, she blessed me.

"Guard over this little one, dear Father."

I went into my house and said hello to Mommy.

"Where have you been so long, Emmie? I was so sad, and I was praying for you. I thought you were lost."

"I don't know. I did get lost, but now I'm home."

Seventeen

Oh! Holy Night

Joe's mother, Mrs. Dorster, asked me to sing in the Little Angels choir at her church. We started to practice three times a week for the Christmas pageant. On Monday, Wednesday and Friday afternoons, she would come and pick me up at home. Mrs. Dorster had a Ford Woody station wagon with plenty of seats. It had three rows and a storage area. I was the first one she picked up. Mrs. Dorster would park in front of a house and honk the horn. A child would run out. Then we'd open the door, and they'd crawl to the back. Soon as the boy or girl was seated, Mrs. Dorster would drive away. She didn't stop until she had the car full of children.

One of the elders would meet us at the front of the church to escort us up to the stage. I couldn't say that it was an altar like in a Catholic church, but the preacher talked about God up there. So it was a holy place. The piano player was an older man, very tall, who wore a grey suit and tie every day. I liked to watch his fingers move on the keys. He could spread his fingers wide open like a fan and cover almost all the ivories. He always started us off with a fast and lively song to get us going. The piano player's wife was up on stage in front of us, raising her arms and pointing her fingers at kids who were too quiet. She was tall like her husband, and she always wore her hair in a French twist with fancy hairpins. Every night at practice, she wore a

72

navy blue skirt and pale blue blouse. She told us when to breathe and when to be quiet. Mr. and Mrs. Penning called each other dear during practice.

"Dear, get the children to hold their high notes a little longer."

"Yes, dear. Could you come in stronger in the beginning?"

"Of course, dear."

Sometimes, I could see Mr. Penning wink at Mrs. Penning, and she'd get all flustered.

"Now, what song were we on children? Oh, I remember."

Joe had a great voice for a boy. He sounded almost like a grown man. Mrs. Penning gave him a solo during practice. She made him come out to the front of the stage by himself. Then Mr. Penning would play a strong and forceful song, and the words Joe sang made me get a lump in my throat. I sniffed my nose and wiped my eyes while Joe was singing. I always felt like I was going to Heaven then. I could see all of us children climbing up a long ladder and singing all the way.

"Let us in, oh Lord, let us in!"

Mr. Penning then played a tune that was low and quiet. We swayed back and forth, our whole group humming.

"Gloria Gloria, Lord Oh Lord."

It was time to leave then. I had my song sheets, and I practiced them on the front porch after supper. It was cold and that meant I could hear whether I sounded good or bad. I think I sounded pretty good. One night, when it wasn't a practice night, Mrs. Dorster came and measured me for a robe. She made me stand still while she had me stick out my arms for my sleeve length. She measured around my shoulders and from head to toe. She measured every part of me. Even my head was wrapped with that tape measure. Mrs. Dorster's sister was there and wrote down all the numbers in a notebook.

"We're going to Wasson's Department Store for the fabric; white satin with grosgrain ribbons for your hair. Every child is going to have an identical robe. You sure will look like little angels on that stage!"

The pageant was two days before Christmas. At our final rehearsal, Mrs. Dorster had each of us try on the new robes. She laughed when Joe tried his on. He was getting bigger and bigger every day. The neck was too tight. She raised her voice a little, but she wasn't mean.

"You won't be able to sing with your neck all twisted like that. I'm going to have to cut the opening still wider. And no more biscuits until Christmas!"

Mr. and Mrs. Penning made us practice how to walk and stand still as a group. They demonstrated how to sit down and then stand up properly. They also showed us how to bow if anyone clapped for us. On pageant night, the church was full. Some people even stood in the back against the wall. I only thought about it once, that I was the only white girl in the choir.

Mr. Penning began to play the piano, just a little background music until everyone sat down. Mrs. Penning came out and gave the introduction, and I forgot what color my skin was. I was part of the Little Angels Choir. I hummed and sang all the right words. I clapped and rang bells with the other children. When they swayed, I swayed. When Mrs. Penning raised her hands, I raised my voice. And when it was time, I sang low. My favorite song was about the infant Jesus, *What Child Is This?* During some of the lines, I sang louder than usual, and I could tell Mrs. Penning was watching me.

"This child, this child of Mary!"

I sang the word Mary as loud as I could. When Joe gave his solo and I forgot that other people were there. It seemed like he was the only person in the church, and I was listening from far away. I began crying, and the girl next to me wiped my tears with her sleeve. We swayed and marched in a group, in union, praising and singing in the House of the Lord. All the people started standing and clapping for the final. They yelled "More! More!" But we exited the stage. Then Mr. Penning played a solo on his piano. We waited until he finished. Suddenly, he called each of us children by name on his microphone. When I heard my name, I went out to join the choir. We stood in a line across the stage and bowed together. Mrs. Penning then raised her hand to signal our final number.

"Silent Night, Holy Night, All is calm, All is bright..."

Out the window, where the morning light shined on me the first time, appeared a scene of twinkling stars. The sky was dark blue, not black like other nights. One star was brighter than the other stars. We children looked up over the people's heads. We sang to the sky that watched over us.

"Holy Infant so tender and mild. Sleep in Heavenly Peace, Sleep in Heavenly Peace..."

The Little Angels Choir then marched off the stage to take off our white robes. We began giggling and teasing one another as we changed back into our dresses and our ordinary clothes.

"You said Thee instead of Thou."

"So, you forgot a whole verse."

"Well, you went high instead of low."

The choir went out to join the reception. I sat on a chair with a plate of rye toast with cheese and olives and little fish cakes to dip in cocktail sauce. Joe's mama came over and handed me a cup of lime sherbet punch and gingerbread with cream cheese icing. I ate everything that was on my plate, and if anyone filled it, I ate again. It wasn't food that made me so happy. It was being there with the people in the House of the Lord.

Eighteen

In The Still of the Night

It snowed on Christmas Eve. Mommy had to work, so Janey and I watched television until she came home. I had an idea to give Cissy a bath in the kitchen sink. I tested the water with my elbow to see if it was warm. She laughed when I scrubbed her head. The bubbles blew all around the kitchen when Cissy slapped the water. I held her while she swam around in the sink for a few minutes. She stood there shivering while I dried her all over. There was so much water on the floor.

"Janey, come mop the kitchen. Cissy spilled water from her bath."

"When the commercial comes on, Emmie. I'm watching *Frosty the Snowman*."

I carried Cissy into the bedroom and put her gown on. She followed me into the kitchen while I made popcorn. First, I melted the grease and added the kernels to the pan while I turned up the heat. When the corn started to pop, I put the lid on. We had a big metal pot with two black handles. I grabbed them with potholders and shook hard until every piece of corn was popped. Janey came into the kitchen then because of the smell. I dumped all the popcorn into a dishpan and added salt and melted butter.

"Let me stir it, please Emmie!" Janey begged.

I gave them both their own small bowl of popcorn. We carried it into the living room with the green Kool-Aid I'd made. Janey thought it was a Christmas drink. We arranged it all on the coffee table in front of us. Cissy sat by me and ate from both her bowl and mine. There were many children's shows on that night. My favorite was the Dick Clark music special. When that was over, we watched a movie, *Miracle on 34th Street*.

About ten o'clock, the people upstairs came home. They made a lot of noise going up the stairs. Billy, the little boy, got a tricycle for Christmas. I know, because he kept saying TRIKE! TRIKE! Then he rode it around and around on the wooden floor. He was directly on top of our living room. Cissy was asleep by then, so I carried her to bed. Janey stretched out and put her head on my lap, but she kept scooting toward the floor. She liked to watch television upside down. Then the people upstairs started yelling.

"You bitch!"

"Quiet. You're drunk!"

"Get me some whiskey, dimwit!"

I didn't know who the other man's voice belonged to. Only a man and a woman and their son lived up there. The voices became louder. I turned up the sound a little so we could hear the movie. The little boy still rode his tricycle on the upstairs floor. I ran to the bathroom to get some cotton balls to put in our ears. The man and the woman kept yelling at each other. That stranger was still talking about whiskey. Janey started crying because it was so noisy. I hurried to shut Cissy's door so she wouldn't wake up, or I'd never get her back to sleep until Mommy came home. Our windows rattled when the people upstairs fell against a wall.

"How could you do that?"

I heard two men's voices then yelling at each other about the woman. Then the woman said something.

"Why are you jealous? You know he doesn't mean anything to me."

The tricycle's wheels were squeaking then as if they were right on our ceiling. Then I heard Billy cry out, "Momma, lookie me!"

Janey had her head under the sofa cushions, and I wrapped a towel around

77

my head to try and stop the noise from sounding louder and louder. On TV, the little girl was sitting on Santa's lap. All around her, people were smiling. Upstairs, the floorboards popped each time someone took another step. It sounded like thunder coming from that apartment. One of the men slapped the woman on the face. I heard his hand hit her cheek. Then she screamed and ran across the floor to hit him back. Billy was crying hard, still riding his tricycle around over our heads.

That's when I heard a gunshot. It was like when you watch television, only louder, clearer. Someone up there fell to the floor. I looked up to see our ceiling light was rocking back and forth, the bulbs flickering as the globes spun around from their chains. The walls shook and caused Mommy's clock to fall off the mantle. Our Daddy's picture crashed down on the brick hearth.

"AHHHHH! You've killed him!"

It was the woman speaking now. She was talking to the other man, the strange visitor.

"You've killed him! You've killed him!"

She kept repeating the same thing until the man spoke back to her.

"Shut up! I'll only say this one time. You'll forever keep your lips closed. Hear me?"

But the man wasn't talking loud like her husband did. The other man used a normal voice that came through the register grate, talking about whiskey again. I could hear someone getting ice cubes out of the freezer and dropping the cubes into their glasses. There was silence. Nobody spoke for a long time. I turned off the television and the lights. Janey and I sat in the dark, watching the street light shine into the room. It made a path of light to Cissy's room. I tiptoed over to her door and peeked through the keyhole. She was curled up in a ball, holding her stuffed rabbit in her arms. Tiger, our cat, came and rubbed against my legs. I picked him up and went back to Janey. The stranger stirred the woman's drink and told her what to do.

"Drink this. Swallow these pills, and you'll be able to relax. Now we have to figure out what to do with the body."

The woman didn't say a word. I thought I heard her sigh. The register was right over our sofa. I leaned over to the side and looked up at the bottoms of her shoes. She must have been sitting at her kitchen table. Once, I took her mail upstairs, and she let me in her kitchen so I knew where her table was. I noticed the open register on the floor, and I knew that if you looked down, anyone could see into our living room. They sat in silence upstairs while Janey and I drank the rest of our Christmas Kool-Aid downstairs. Way in the back of the house, I could hear Billy crying. He stopped after a while. Mommy woke us up after midnight when she came home from work. She had ham sandwiches leftover from a special party. The three of us sat around the coffee table dipping our sandwiches into the little cups of mustard and horseradish sauce. There were coconut cookies and spiced apples for dessert. We had a glass of eggnog with cinnamon on top, and then Mommy told us we had to go to sleep.

Nobody upstairs said anything else, and I never told Mommy what happened. I had picked up her clock and put it back on the mantle, and it wasn't broken. Daddy's picture was only chipped on the frame. I kept hoping Mommy wouldn't notice. He smiled out at us while we had our midnight supper. I liked that picture. It was the one where he was working in his garden, and the corn stalks were as tall as he was. I thought about planting corn all night. Put three kernels and a bean down into a little hole, next cover them up with your fingers. Make rows and save room to walk through them. The corn will grow up, and the beans will wind around the stalks. Make good use of the earth, and you will have something in return. All night long, I dreamed of Daddy bent over as he planted corn.

Next morning, I got out of bed real early. The snow had stopped during the night, and the air was cold and still. Out in the backyard, I looked for clues. I was on the side of the house when I heard two voices, two men talking about moving something heavy. I poked my head around the corner of the house. I saw the stranger, the one with the rough voice who kept wanting more whiskey. When he spoke, I knew it was him. The other man must have been his brother because he looked like him. But his voice was different, louder. They had greasy black hair combed back and puffy faces with holes in their skin. They looked like they didn't belong in the neighborhood. We had lots of different people from many countries, but those men seemed like they were from a strange place. They were short with big shoulders, and I thought that their clothes were weird. The men in our city didn't wear pants like that, and their shoes looked like they came from somewhere else. I saw a movie once about a group of thieves in New York, and they had on clothes like the two men. That was it. They weren't from Indianapolis. They were from New York!

I had to peek through a hole in the downspout so they wouldn't see me. The two men were pushing a large cardboard box that said GE REFRIGERATOR. I didn't want them to know that I was there, so I kept quiet. I held my breath and then blew out air into my mittens. I pulled back my earmuff so I could hear what they said. I was cold, but I stood still. It was Christmas morning, seven o'clock, and nobody was up yet except me. No neighbors were out, and no one walked down the street. The men opened the cellar door. You could go down into the cellar from the outside. It was a different part of the house that nobody ever went to, just some rooms with old furniture and junk metal parts. I went down there once and saw hooks hanging from the ceiling and some wooden tables. Mommy said that people used to hang meat down there and pour salt on it to cure, and that they stored vegetables and fruits for the winter. I already knew what it looked like down there where the men were going.

One of the men pushed the box while the other pulled. It got stuck on the stairs, and they tried to lift it up. Something inside the box made a whooshing sound as it slid inside the cardboard to the bottom part of the box. The man at the end said he couldn't hold it any longer. They cussed and said every bad word I had ever heard. I could hear when they finally got the box unstuck from the wooden stairs.

"Damn piece of wood. A splinter!"

The other man grunted as he pushed the box completely down to the bottom of the cellar. I heard them groaning and taking deep breaths like they were working so hard. When I knew they were in the room downstairs over in the side room, I tiptoed to the door and looked in. There were drops of blood on the steps. I ran back to the side of the house to think of what to do. I looked down at my feet, and there were red spots on the ground. My hands were cold, and nobody was awake yet. I tiptoed silently back around to the front of the house and went in the front door. Mommy was still asleep, so I read the telephone book until she woke up. We had oatmeal and hot tea for breakfast. I knew the men in the cellar stayed down there all day not speaking, waiting for night to come.

Daddy came over and took us to Shapiro's restaurant. I ordered Swiss steak and looked around at all the people. He said it was the most expensive item on the menu, but it was okay. It was a holiday.

"When you're dead, you don't get to eat anymore."

"Why do you say that, Emmie?" Daddy asked me.

"I'm just very happy to be eating right now. Can I have cherry pie and ice cream?"

We all ate our Christmas dinner, and then we walked around the Circle. Every year, the city decorated it. Little elves made toys for Santa in one display. In another, wooden soldiers marched and played music. I saw dancers gliding over the ice, twirling around and around. A choir dressed in red velvet robes and fur hats sang about Jesus and his birth. We stopped at the place where the Holy Family rested. Mary knelt beside the newborn Jesus while Joseph stood guard with the Angels. Animals and the Wise Men came to adore Him, the Child of God. Families strolled and smiled at each other. All around, there were red ribbons and twinkling lights on all the buildings. I looked up at the monument. It was lit up like a giant Christmas tree. The star at the top shined the brightest. The air was clear, and the moon was full, lighting up the entire Circle. Christmas night was beautiful.

Daddy drove us home, and we hugged him goodbye. We opened our presents that Daddy left on our doorstep. Cissy got a clown doll with red hair and freckles. Janey's gift was a paint set, and Mommy got a new fuzzy robe. My box was so heavy that Mommy had to help me carry it. We sat it down in the middle of the living room floor, and I tore off the wrapping paper. Inside was a set of encyclopedias-*The Countries of the World*. I sat down to look at all the pictures first. It was quiet in the cellar and the upstairs. Mommy walked into the living room and waved a piece of paper around.

"Look what I found taped to the back door. It's from the woman upstairs.

She says they moved out and to let the landlord know that they are all paid up. He can keep their deposit. Well, people are strange, moving on Christmas Day!"

I kept reading my books. The country of China was interesting. I would go there someday. I thought of little Billy and wondered if his mother remembered to take his tricycle when they moved out. I sat there on the floor, under the spot where Billy rode around upstairs. The house was quiet, and we had all the lights on. I kept reading until Mommy said to stop or I would go blind. We turned on the little electric candle in the front window when we went to bed.

I fell asleep thinking about Billy. That other man who drank all the whiskey was probably his Daddy now. I thought I heard Billy crying, but I couldn't have. He was gone from upstairs. Cissy made a sound in her sleep, and I closed my eyes. Billy had a new house far away. He rode around and around all day on his tricycle, and his mother smiled at him. And I hoped Billy's new Daddy never hurt him or his mother.

Nineteen

In Your Eyes

∼⟨ co⟩∼

J oe was waiting for me that first morning after Christmas vacation.

"This is for you. I went to Alabama with Mama and I found something for you."

He stuck out his hand to me and opened up his fingers. In the center of his palm was a seashell. It was the size of a tennis ball, one of those shells that you hold up to your ear and listen to the ocean.

"Can you hear it? Can you hear the water?"

I put the pink edge of the shell close to my ear and closed my other ear with my finger.

"Now close your eyes, Emmie!"

The waves crashed on the beach far away. It was a cold morning with the sun rising over the horizon. I could see Joe wearing a striped shirt and jeans rolled up to his chubby knees. He was bent over, picking up every shell on the beach, examining all of them until he found the perfect one. His mama walked and walked with her yellow beach dress blowing around her ankles. She found a smooth spot in the sand and spread a tablecloth. She took biscuits, boiled eggs and apricot preserves from her bag. I watched her break apart a biscuit and pile it high with butter and preserves. Joe ran over and sat down on the sand beside her, taking the biscuit from his Mama's hand. They sipped hot coffee and milk with brown sugar while they looked out over the waves. A ship passed and blew its horn, then turned and went out to sea. Joe's Mama held the shell up to her ear and smiled. When they finished their breakfast, they drove back to Indiana. Their car was all loaded up with seashells and sand.

"I can hear the ocean, Joe. It's strong and the wind is blowing inside the shell."

"It's for you, Emmie. This is the most perfect shell I could find. My mama said that none could be exactly perfect 'cause God makes them just like people. Every person has some flaws like the shells. She said some might be beautiful on the outside but full of rotten stuff inside, and others might be plain on the outside and yet make the prettiest music if you listen hard. I think this one's like you-strong and shiny with the wind blowing all around you and a little covering of grit and sand. See! It's pink and white and those are your colors. It's my Christmas gift to you."

I didn't have a present for Joe, so I told him the story of what happened on Christmas Eve. He listened with all his attention to every detail. Every sound effect I made, he jumped or covered his ears. When my story was over, he shook my hand.

"I will never tell another person as long as I live. Thanks for telling me. I promise."

Then to break the tension, I also told him the story in the Bible, the story of the real Christmas Eve. I knew that he had already heard the story because his mother was so religious. They went to the House of the Lord every Sunday and Thursday evening. But he listened anyway.

"And that is the most beautiful story in the world."

Joe always liked to put a comment in at the end of every conversation. School would be starting soon, so we hurried to everyone's house.

"Merry Christmas! Happy New Year!"

George bowed to Joe and me. Janey was behind and imitated George. He saw her, but he didn't get mad because he thought it was funny. Lots of things made George laugh. Polly ran out to meet us with new green earrings on. They were diamond shaped and sparkled like the rest of her. When we got to school, there was a large sign in the hallway.

SPELLING BEE—SIGN UP NOW!

The woman at the desk asked us our names and wrote them on her list. She stared at us as if we were strange, but then the woman shook our hands.

"The competition is in one month. Come to the meeting after school. May the best man or woman win!"

George kept smiling to himself all day like he had a secret. It was good to be back in school.

Twenty

Dream On

E very day, I drilled my friends with the spelling words.

"How do you spell freedom?"

"I know!" It was George.

"F-r-e-e-d-o-m!" He yelled out each letter in a loud voice.

People passed by the front porch and stared at George, but he didn't care. I gave him another word.

"VIGILANCE."

Joe answered correctly and then used both words in a sentence.

"The price of freedom is vigilance."

"Polly," I turned to her, "spell the word eternal."

She stood up on the front step and looked out at the street. A woman walking by just then stopped to listen to Polly.

"E-T-E-R-N-A-L. The works of good men are eternal."

The woman put down her sack of groceries and clapped for Polly, then went on her way. That caused Polly to stand and take a bow like George sometimes did. Other days, we went to the Central Public Library and read every dictionary that we could find. Each one of us had a stack of books in front of us. As one child closed a book, the other grabbed it from the stack.

We passed all the dictionaries around the table on the final practice day. The librarian came to us and said that the library was closing. I looked up at the big clock above my head. We had asked permission from our parents to stay until 9:00, and it was dark outside. It was a Friday in late February as the four of us stepped out into the night. George started chattering his teeth, so I started running with all the rest following me. I could hear Joe's heavy puffing far behind me, and Polly's light heels clicking fast on the sidewalk. I knew George was with us. The sound of his corduroy pants rubbed together at the knees. Polly started the laughing first and then the rest of us. I don't know what was funny, but the four of us laughed while we ran. I ran faster and faster, and they tried to catch me. My brown school shoes were good to run in. I stopped for a second to see if no cars were coming, then I ran across the street. They each did the same. It was cold and quiet, and there was no one outside but us children. We barely reached George's house when it started snowing. That's when I gave my final orders to the group.

"Bye George! Bye Joe! Bye Polly! Dress warm in the morning. Meet you on the corner at 7:00 am."

I ran again all the way to my house. Mommy was holding the door open, all the lights burning in our house.

"I made chicken pot pies. Yours is in the oven still warm. Cissy's asleep and Janey's in the tub. Be back about midnight. I just need to make a few dollars for the electric bill."

Then Mommy kissed me hard on the cheek. I rubbed off the lipstick and went to get my pot pie. Janey came into the kitchen all wet and wrapped in a towel.

"What are you doing, Emmie? Are you reading?"

"I'm studying and writing down all the words I know how to spell."

"Well, you must know a lot of them 'cause you already have two hundred! How many words are there in the world?"

"No one can count them, Janey. People make new words every day."

"Do you know how to spell my favorite word?"

"What is it?"

"Sister!"

I spelled it for her, and she grinned.

"When we get big, Emmie, will you still be my sister?"

"Of course, silly! We'll be the same, but our bodies will be old."

"Then we can still eat pot pies and listen to Top Ten Countdown on the radio?"

"You can bet on it, Janey."

I watched her eat every bite of chicken out of her little pie pan. Mommy made delicious pot pies, better than the frozen kind. She put potatoes, peas, and little pieces of red pepper and celery. The crust was flaky and golden brown. Janey tipped her pan up to her mouth and drank all the gravy. She started to shake a little since she was wearing only a towel.

"You stay here and write, Emmie. I already covered Cissy up. I'll get my pajamas on. I'm getting big now."

Janey kissed me and wrapped her wet arms around my neck.

"Goodnight, Emmie. I love you!"

"Goodnight, Janey. I love you too!"

At the top of my page, I wrote *Sisters Forever—Janey, Cissy and Emmie.*

Janey smiled so wide, you could see her missing tooth in the front.

"Dry yourself good! Don't sleep in that old wet towel."

I couldn't resist telling her what to do.

Twenty-One

Freedom for My People

❦

Everyone met me on the corner the next morning just like I told them. Joe pulled out a fried egg sandwich for each one of us. I unwrapped the wax paper to take a look. His mom had put chopped pickles with mayonnaise and ketchup on the bread. George really liked his sandwich so much that I had to wipe the egg from his chin.

"Thank you, Joe. Now I can be really happy."

Polly reached out her hand to shake Joe's. You should have seen him. He always looked so good and helpful when he smiled like that. We were the first students to arrive, so the janitor let us sit in the auditorium. Mr. Ramsey came in about 8:30.

"Come help me set up the stage, kids."

He had George and Joe set up a row of chairs facing the audience. I plugged in the microphone while Polly dusted the lectern and the chairs. Mr. Ramsey and the janitor carried a desk up on the stage for the teacher in charge. We had forty students in the contest. Each one of them took a seat in the first few rows. About ten minutes to nine, some spectators came in, mostly parents and teachers. I turned around to count them all, and I guessed there were close to a hundred adults. Even a few students who were not in the competition came to see us. It was after nine o'clock and I waited eagerly for the contest to begin.

"Ladies and gentlemen! Welcome! This is the Eight Annual Spelling Competition at Indianapolis Public School Number 45. I'm the principal, Mr. Hardy."

A photographer from the Indianapolis Times flashed his camera in our direction.

"I would like to introduce Mr. Ramsey, 6th-grade teacher. He will be the moderator of this contest."

I looked at Mr. Ramsey to see if he made any special speeches. He said one word since he was a sort of quiet person.

"Thanks."

The first round was girls against boys. Polly did great for three turns, but then the word "avarice" came up. It was a rule that the contestant could take sixty seconds and ask to hear the word again three times.

"Come on Polly! A-V-A-R-I-C-E."

She couldn't hear me, but I was screaming the letters inside my head. I didn't want to get her kicked out of the contest.

"Correct, Polly."

She had spelled the word right. Mr. Ramsey read her name off the tag we all wore and went immediately to the next person.

"Conglomeration." Joe got that one.

"Abhorrent" George knew that one.

"Gestation."

That was a perfect word for me since I had just read about the birth of horses. The girls competed against each other and also the group of boys. At the end of the rounds, the leading students were listed on the board for the whole audience to see. There were five names—Polly, George, Joe, Emmie, and Walter. Walter was a smart guy who wore thick eyeglasses. Every day, he finished his assignments early. He never spoke unless you asked him a question. He'd answer, but he didn't say any extra words. If you needed a pencil or a sheet of paper, or if you forgot to bring an eraser, you could always get what you needed from him. Mr. Ramsey always said, "Ask Walter."

At 10:45, the teachers gave us an intermission to go to the bathroom. Some of the mothers had a table set up in the hallway with pastries and juice. At 11:15, the bell rang, and Mr. Hardy made an announcement over the loudspeaker.

"Final round of the spelling competition. Now!"

I hurried back up on the stage and took my seat next to Polly. I looked out and saw Janey waving at me. Mommy had come to see me spell words.

"Hi, Baby!" She mouthed the words but I understood.

I tucked in my blouse into my skirt and pulled up my socks all the way to my knees.

"Each student has five minutes to spell ten words," Mr. Ramsey instructed us.

Joe was the first. He spelled eight words correctly, but "statuary" got him. He still smiled real big as he passed by me to go down off the stage.

"Good luck" he whispered.

Polly took her time. She didn't seem rushed by the ticking clock. She just stood up straight and spelled every word that she was given. On the seventh, she misspelled "malinger." When she bowed to the spectators, there was lots of clapping. And of course, she twirled her skirt around for all the people to see. I felt sad for her when she left me up there with George and Walter.

I was next. Peruse, Antipathy, Voluminous. Each word made me stop and think hard before I tried to spell it. On the ninth word, Ocelot, I thought I had it right. I put an extra "c" in, and Mr. Ramsey let me know.

"I am sorry, Emmie. But you are now out of the contest. Take your seat with the others."

I walked off the stage and sat down next to Joe and Polly right in front. Walter spelled all his words right and so did George. It was a tie. Mr. Ramsey whispered with some other teachers, and they decided that George and Walter would have to spell five more words correctly to break the tie. George was led off the stage out to the hall by the principal. He didn't want George to hear the list of words. Walter spelled them all correctly. When George came back, he also spelled them the right way.

This went on for three rounds, and nobody could break the tie. Mr. Hardy had the idea of letting a student choose a word. We each wrote our names on a piece of paper and stuffed it into a box that was passed from row to row. Mr. Ramsey stirred all the names in the box. He shook it and turned it upside down.

There was silence in the gymnasium. Everyone whispered who would be picked. It was like a contest between all the students just to have their name said out loud.

"Emmie O'Brien!"

I stood up and slowly climbed the steps toward Mr. Ramsey.

"Emmie, choose a word and ask each contestant to use it in a sentence."

Many words floated around in my mind, each of them trying to be the tiebreaker. I looked at Walter with his pencils sticking out of his shirt pocket. He was standing still and had his hands clasped together. I had never noticed before that his skin was pink and I studied the part in his brown hair. There was my friend George, smiling wide and his shiny black hair combed back from his eyes so he could see. He had on his black pants and white shirt, the same as every day, but there was something different about him that morning. He was wearing a pin of the American flag on his collar.

"Allegiance."

Walter stuttered, "A-LL-ALL-EEGENCE."

"Could you use the word in a sentence?" I asked him.

He stuttered some more, taking the pencils from his pocket and putting them back again.

"Allegiance is…is..allegiance is..I don't know!"

The audience was quiet as Walter slowly returned to his seat with the other students. Mr. Hardy led George back into the gym and up the steps. He stared straight out into the crowd. I asked George how to spell the word allegiance and to put in into a sentence.

"A-L-L-E-G-I-A-N-C-E!"

He got it right the first time. How proud he looked as I watched him recite.

"I pledge allegiance to the flag and to the United States of America…"

There was the flag draped down on the wall in the back of the auditorium. Why hadn't I noticed it before? The entire group of spectators stared up at

George as he saluted the flag. I stood beside him and put my hand over my heart just as George did. When he finished, he turned to Mr. Ramsey and bowed slightly from the waist.

"You're the winner! George Washington is the number one speller of IPS Number 45."

Mr. Ramsey let me hang the gold medal around George's neck. It was so heavy and George was so little, that the medal hung down to his belt. Mr. Hardy gave George a framed certificate with his name written by Angela Small, the student with the neatest handwriting. The reporter from the newspaper interviewed George for the paper. A photographer snapped his picture. George was still wearing that medal around his neck.

"I must thank my fellow student, Emmie, for helping me study many words."

Later that afternoon, I saw George's picture in the Indianapolis Times newspaper paper. He was smiling and holding his certificate. Under the picture, there was a caption that he was so proud of, "Chinese Immigrant Wins Spelling Bee."

George's father brought a copy of the paper to every house in the neighborhood. He laughed and laughed so hard as he walked away.

Twenty-Two

When We Were Young

❦

March was cold that year. Early one Saturday, I woke up to the sound of someone out in the hall.

"Get up, get up little sleepyheads! We are going skating."

Daddy was standing there holding a pair of skates with shiny blades.

"Ice skates? Where are we going?" I asked him.

I put on every bit of clothing I owned— shorts on top of pajama bottoms. Mommy's hose under my socks and a dress on top of everything else.

"I'm ready now."

"Put your sweater on under your coat and wear my hat."

Daddy tied a scarf around my neck. We had to find something for Janey to wear. I put two undershirts on her and then Mommy's long-sleeved blouse. Next, I put her pajama top back on her and two pairs of socks. I made Janey wear Mommy's Bermuda shorts on top of her pajama bottoms. The shorts were light blue and long so, they looked like pants anyway. We didn't look too bad after all. I buttoned Janey's coat but made her tie her own saddle oxfords. Just then, Daddy pulled out a new pair of pink earmuffs from his pocket and put them on Janey's head.

"Mommy, we're going skating with Daddy. Cissy can't go since she's too little."

I ran to kiss Mommy. She was sitting in bed, holding the baby.

"We'll be fine. I've got to wash Cissy's diapers in the bathtub anyway. I'll be busy."

Daddy pulled out two pairs of work gloves from his pocket and gave Janey and me a pair. I went over to the table to see what was in the sack he brought. It was full of donut sticks from the Wonder Bread outlet. Janey and I stuffed our pockets full and went down to get in Daddy's car. Before Daddy drove away, he gave us each a few sips of hot tea from his thermos.

It was snowing when we parked by the edge of Fall Creek. I looked down at the water and there were all my neighbors. Every kid in school came to skate that day. Daddy opened the car door and we rolled down the hill that was covered in snow. When we landed at the bottom, Janey and I made snow angels. Daddy ran so fast, he was out on the ice before we were. I sat on a log to put on the white leather skates. They had long laces that wrapped around my ankles.

"Stand up! Let me tie them or you'll fall down."

I held on to Daddy's shoulder while he pulled the laces tight. They were just the right size. Janey was already gliding around on the frozen creek with her shoes on. I would let her try my new skates, but first I had to go fast out in the middle of the ice. My legs were wobbly, yet if I leaned forward, I could skate. Daddy grabbed my hands and we went from one end of the ice to the other. I followed Daddy and Janey down to the bridge where Polly was skating.

"Do this, Emmie!"

Her hair whirled around and she raised her arms up to the sky.

"I can't do that."

"Yes, you can. Try it now!"

Polly skated all around me in a circle, her skirt blowing out from behind her like a cape. She made a figure eight then she spelled her own name in the ice with the blade of her skates. With outstretched arms, she twirled so fast, that I felt dizzy.

"Where'd you learn how to skate like that, Polly? You look like those girls in the competitions."

She spun around one more time and came closer.

"There was a young woman from our village in Romania. She went to high school in Bucharest because she was a good skater. She won gold medals and came back every Saturday to teach the other children. Now, you try it like I did!"

But all I could do was to go straight and fast from one side of the creek to the other. When I tried to twirl, I fell down on my bottom. Polly pulled me up and spun me around with one arm. The people flew past me. There was Daddy by the side. Janey looked blurry and all my friends watched from the hill. How fast the snowflakes were falling. They spun and fluttered all around my face. George was laughing, Joe was waving, and all the neighbors smiled as we passed by. We carved circles in the ice with our blades, turned left and right and made zigzags. Polly held my hand and we started spinning.

"98! 99! 100!" the crowd chanted.

I laughed out loud then and yelled, "We did it!"

But I never could have made one hundred circles without Polly helping. I had to sit down on the creek bank to catch my breath. Polly waved and then skated away. I took off my skates to let Janey wear them. How funny she looked, falling down each time she got up. I got behind her and pushed her all the way to the bridge where some people were gathered. Mr. Penning, the piano player from church, was talking to the group.

"We are having a race. First one to the other bridge wins. Who wants to be in it?"

I grabbed my skates back from Janey. When the whistle blew, I took off. Bending forward from the waist, I put my head down like I was running on the sidewalk. The wind stung my eyes but I kept going. People on both sides bumped into me and I continued skating. My lips were freezing. I just put one skate in front of the other and pushed hard. I was flying! I was almost there. Some of the people quit, but not me. Then I hit a bump in the ice, and I fell on my arm. My glove came off one hand, and I slid on my side toward the finish line. But not quite.

"Get up, Emmie. You can do it!"

Polly ran along the edge of the creek cheering me.

"Skate! Skate faster!"

I got up and pushed, flying on my skates toward the bridge. Polly cheered and screamed.

"Go faster! Yeah! Yeah! Yeah! Faster! Faster!"

It seemed like she was giving me strength by her yelling. I had to win since she was calling me so loud.

"There are only four behind you. Keep going!"

I turned my head for a second and saw George's father and Mr. Ogre's son coming after me, the big, ugly kid with those pointy teeth and nose like a beak. He was coming to get me. Daddy was skating behind me.

"You're almost there, Emmie. Go! Go! Go! Don't stop! Win, win, win!"

My heart was beating as fast as Polly shouted her words. The bridge was so close. I kept skating. Then Daddy flew past me and touched the foot of the bridge with his skate. He was the winner! I skated to meet him. Mr. Penning called out our names.

"Number one is Mr. O'Brien. Number two is Emmie O'Brien. Number three is Mr. Washington. And in final place, Daniel Ogre."

I sat down on a large rock, still wearing my skates, and I watched all the neighbors clapping. The crowd stood there on the bank of the water. Some people had their thermos jugs filled with hot coffee, and they offered a cup to anyone who looked cold. I saw George's grandma carrying a white cloth rolled up into a package. She would go up to someone, take something from inside, and hand it to them. Whatever it was, the person tasted it and smiled. She went from person to person, pulling out pieces of something from her bundle. I started to go see what she was giving out when Polly skated up to me, stopping at my feet.

"You're a winner."

"I'm number two."

"But two is a winner. Your father was faster but you finished. Your name was in the winner's group!"

"You're right, Polly. Next time, can you teach me how to do figure 8s all by myself ?"

"Sure, Emmie, next time the water becomes ice."

Daddy was waiting for us at the top of the hill.

"Are you hungry girls? I know where we can get the best pork tenderloin sandwiches."

The only thing for sale at Gadonski's on New York Street was raw meat and cooked tenderloins. Janey and I each got our own sandwich wrapped in wax paper. The huge slice of breaded pork meat was bigger than the bun. I lifted the top of my bun to see if they added mayonnaise and sweet pickles. The steam rose up to my face as I took a bite. Mr. Gadonski and his wife watched us eat their tenderloins. When they were convinced that we liked the taste, they both smiled.

"Have a Nehi?"

Mr. Gadonski held up bottles of colored pop from his ice chest. Janey grabbed the grape flavor and Daddy took the orange one. There was one bottle of clear cream soda so I asked for that. Mrs. Gadonski popped the bottles open on the side of the chest. Janey sat on the window ledge to finish her drink.

"I suppose you should order your mother a tenderloin. Here's sixty cents, Emmie."

Mrs. Gadonski wrapped it up in double wax paper and stuffed it into a paper bag. The bell above the door rang as we left the shop. It wasn't snowing anymore. I kissed Daddy on the cheek and Janey gave him a hug before he drove away.

Twenty-Three

Learning to Fly

G eorge's father was standing outside the school building one day as we left. It was the middle of March. The wind was blowing on that bright day and just a little cold. He had his gray tweed coat buttoned all the way up to his neck, and he stood there without moving. He smiled at us and we waved. George walked politely up to his father. They whispered in Chinese for a few seconds. Our group stood and waited because George's father had come to school. Maybe it was something important. Then George walked over to us.

"My father has a new toy that he made. He would like you to come with us to try it."

George said all the right words in the right order.

"OKAY!" I decided. "We'll go with you."

We followed Mr. Washington the few blocks to the creek. Only a few weeks before, we had skated on frozen ice. Now, the water gurgled and splashed on the rocks as it flowed south to White River. I held Janey's hand, but she wanted to roll down the hill like we did when Daddy brought us. I let go of her, and she went spinning down. George thought that was fun, so he did what Janey did. We had never heard George laugh that hard before. Next, I rolled down the hill and landed on top of them. There were yellow daffodils and white crocuses popping out of the muddy ground. Janey spotted the first robin redbreast sitting on a tree stump. The bird had a mouthful of worms. Janey tried to get closer, but the robin flew up to another tree where she had her nest We could hear baby birds peeping and chirping as the mother bird fed them worms.

Mr. Washington unbuttoned his coat and took out a wooden stick. It had red and white paper wrapped around it, and it was tied with string. I looked at Polly. Her eyes were as big as black stones that we picked up from the creek bank. I thought I knew what it was. Then Joe couldn't stand it any longer.

"What is it, Mr. Washington?"

"Kite" he answered in English.

With one gentle shake of his arm, George's father had the paper bird up in the air. The strings were almost invisible. It was a large bird with arms spread wide and a beak turned to the side. It seemed to fly up, high up to the afternoon sun, then spin around in circles, diving down to meet us children.

"Oooh! Look at him flying!" Janey jumped up to touch the bird as he went by.

"He's sitting in the tree!"

"Now he's flapping his wings and flying sideways."

"It's blocking the sun!"

Each of us narrated the show. Mr. Washington moved his hands so easy like he was drawing a painting in the sky with the paper kite. There were puffy clouds in the blue sky. Sometimes, the bird seemed to be sitting on a cloud, or he landed on a rock in the water. Once, a blue heron posed beside the paper bird, and they looked like the best of friends. George's father let each of us try to fly the kite. It was not as easy as it appeared when he did it. The bird fell to the ground and he became tangled up in the tree branches. Janey begged Mr. Washington.

"Make him fly one more time."

"Follow me."

The big red bird flew above our heads as we walked down Pennsylvania Street. Mr. Washington waited until we each went inside our homes before he took the kite down. I looked out the front window to see him roll up the kite and button his coat up to his neck. He turned around and walked home with George.

"You're late, Emmie. I'm needed early."

"I'm sorry, Mommy. George's dad made a paper bird. We went to fly it in the sky."

Cissy made me say the word "bird" over and over, and she wouldn't stop asking. Janey drew a picture of a bird for her so she'd hush for a while. I hung it on the wall above Cissy's bed. The bird was red and white with big wings spread out. Under the bird, there was a small figure of a man waving his arms in the air. He had a smile on his face as he made the bird fly. Cissy loved the picture. She said "ooh" for hours while I did my homework. Janey took a bath and tried to tug the tangles from hair.

"Can we make a kite, Emmie?" I thought for a minute.

"We'll never be able to make a kite like Mr. Washington's. Maybe someday, we'll watch him again."

Janey gave me a hug before she laid her head on the pillow.

"I'm going to look out the window and try to see the bird flying."

She kept her eyes open and turned toward the window. It was dark outside and no paper birds were flying, but I kept the shade up anyway just so Janey could watch for it.

Twenty-Four

Sometimes You Can't Make It on Your Own

We were out of school for spring vacation, and I went over to Polly's house. She joined me for a walk to see George and Joe. They were each sitting on their porches with nothing to do. I suggested that we all go for a walk in the neighborhood. The four of us plus Janey were just walking and having fun when a group of boys came toward us. They were talking real loud, laughing and making a lot of noise. I stopped so that they would pass by our group. But the boys just kept standing still.

"Where are you going?" one of them asked me.

"We're walking around. Why?"

He got real angry when I said that. Something strange happened to him. He began to act differently and to argue with me.

"You can't walk around here. We don't allow no NIGGER LOVERS."

I looked over at Joe. I knew that was a bad name for him because his skin was black. Joe just stood there. I started walking, and the other kids joined me. But the boys in the other group wouldn't let us pass.

"What's a cute white girl like you doing with SLANT-EYES?"

One of the gang pointed at George and pushed his finger into George's chest.

"Yeah! Who said we want FOREIGNERS in this neighborhood? Go back where you came from."

"You better stop hanging around with those not your kind, white girl. You'll regret it. Get what I mean?'

"This dark one'll be nice to take out behind the school and do what we want!"

The boy who said that to Polly was slobbering and spitting the words. He had to wipe his mouth on his sleeve; he was forcing those words out of so fast. Polly didn't understand everything he said to her, but she knew what he meant. She stood still and then he pulled one of her earrings right out of her ear, yanking so hard, her ear started bleeding. I didn't know what to do. One of the earrings rolled down the sidewalk and into the street.

"Can't even talk right, can you CHINK?"

One of them pushed George back, and he fell down since he was so light.

"Stop it! Leave us alone!" I yelled at them.

They wouldn't go away. I tried to help George up, and one of the gang pulled and yanked on my chain.

"Catholic! Pope Lover! You worship the dead! Goin' around with the other kind! What's the matter? You don't like guys like us? Too good for real men?"

He had strange green eyes, the boy who said that. All I could do was watch his eyes as he pulled me closer to him. With his hands clutched around my necklace, he pulled me. My own chain cut into my neck, and I could feel drops of blood running down my chest. His face was just inches away from mine. The air coming out of his mouth felt so hot, and it had a terrible smell like vomit. He knocked me down on the ground, slamming my back on the sidewalk. All the while, he hovered over me screaming and pulling on my Miraculous Medal.

"Take your Virgin Mary and get out of this neighborhood. Catholics don't belong with decent folks."

He was foaming at the mouth like a wild dog with rabies. Some of his hair got caught in my teeth and I spit on the ground. But my medal would not come off me.

"Get her sister!"

Another boy grabbed Janey and ran away. When Joe saw that, he came to life. His big arm reached all the way around the boy's neck and stopped him in his tracks. Janey fell on the sidewalk and rolled away. Polly and George jumped on top of the other boys while I grabbed Janey up in my arms.

"You are not getting my sister!" I screamed.

The weird one came toward me again. His hands were spread out, ready to choke me, but then Polly began to pray the Hail Mary and the Our Father out loud. Her crystal rosary beads glistened in the sun as they hung from her belt loop. She touched the beads and begged Jesus for help. The strange boy stopped and turned around. Without a word, the gang ran into the street as a car was driving by. Janey put her face in my shoulder and cried. It was such a loud noise-the car screeching its tires as it came around the corner and hitting each boy as he ran backward into the street. Then it was silent. The driver got out of the car, and we could tell he was drunk. He staggered over to the curb and sat down. A man walking down the street asked if we were all right.

"Yes. We're okay now," I answered.

"I'm going right away to the drugstore and call the police, kids."

Two of the boys were lying still there in the street, their faces pressed down into the pavement. The weird one had his face turned toward us. His green eyes were glaring directly at me. Now they seemed to be just regular eyes. With the blond hair and plaid shirt, now he looked like all the rest. I watched him just to see if he would get up and come after me, but he never moved. Joe began to hum a gospel tune when the ambulance came. The bodies were all covered up with sheets except the different one. I was scared to see if his eyes ever closed. They never did. Then the paramedics drew a sheet over his head like the others. Joe's mother heard what happened from one of the onlookers, and she came to meet us.

"This is a tragedy, children, on the day of our good Lord's death. This is Good Friday, Holy Friday. On the third day, He will rise again. Pray for the souls of these dead children that they may have asked to be with our Father at the hour of their death. Amen!"

We bowed our heads right there on the corner, Joe still humming that sorrowful song. His mama took us all home to her kitchen where she fed us a meal of fish soup and bread. After lunch, she read us the Easter story from the Bible-the whole story of Jesus' Crucifixion and Resurrection.

"Now, go home and get ready for Easter. Be prepared for the coming of the Lord."

She squeezed each one of us and gave us a colored egg with our name written in crayon. EMMIE. Mine was a beautiful green egg. I held it in one hand and Janey's hand with the other. Mommy didn't have to work that night since there weren't going to be many customers. Everyone was busy getting ready for Easter. Mommy let me paint my fingernails with rose polish. I took artificial flowers out of a basket and placed mine and Janey's eggs inside. Alice came over to give Mommy a permanent. They sat in the kitchen for hours with a pot of coffee. I heard them talking, and they never drank vodka that night.

"Come in here girls. Look at your mom's brand new hairdo."

Alice had put something on Mommy's hair to make it shiny. The curls made her look young and pretty. Cissy crawled up in Mommy's lap.

"Mommy's pretty," Cissy kept saying.

Alice combed Cissy's hair and put powder on her neck and back. Then Janey and I each climbed in Mommy's lap. Alice took a picture of us.

"Do my hair," Janey begged.

Alice washed our hair with egg shampoo and gave us a vinegar rinse. She trimmed our bangs and gave me a facial with a clay mud mask. Cissy laughed at me. I had to sit still until the clay turned hard. Then Alice put a steaming wet towel on my face to soften the clay. When it was soft again, she lightly rubbed all the clay off. She finished by having me hold my face over the kitchen sink while she poured ice water on my skin to seal my pores. For the finish, she applied warm baby oil and dabbed my face with a tissue. She held a mirror up to my face so I could see. I looked the same only my skin was bright pink and shiny, and I did look really clean.

The three of us girls took a bath with some little bottles of oil that Alice brought over. She held the bottles over the running water, and they instantly turned into mountains of pink bubbles. We let Cissy get in first so she could play with the bubbles, and she loved it. Janey was next. I had my own tub of bubbles after they were done. But I only got wet from the neck down. I did not want to ruin my shampooed hair and my clay-softened face. I kept thinking about the boy with those strange green eyes-the one who looked like an ordinary boy one minute and then something happened. His eyes became different and he attacked me. My medal cutting into my skin. Joe's big arms. George trying to jump on one of the boy's back. Polly praying. Rosary beads. The boys running backward. The car. Crash. His eyes back to normal. The sheets.

I was falling asleep in the bathtub. Mommy came in to check on me and made me go to bed. I was so tired when Good Friday was over. As I went to sleep, I held my Miraculous Medal in my hand and looked at the picture of Mary. Her arms were spread out like she was inviting me somewhere or asking me a question. There were twelve stars all around the oval medal, around Mary.

"What can I do?" I wondered.

Then a voice answered inside my head. It sounded like my voice, but it was not. I was listening to something that someone else said. The words were like those of Joe's mother, but it was not her voice. It was clear and strong and urgent. It was an order, and the person spoke with authority, with benevolence.

"Pray for those who do not know the Lord. Ask forgiveness in their names."

I turned my medal over in my hands, and then I slipped it over my head. Alice had put some salve on the raw part where the chain had cut into my skin. I took my hair and put it between the chain and my skin so I couldn't feel the pain too much. Even though nobody said that I had to wear the medal, I liked to have Mary close to me. Janey was already asleep, and I could hear Cissy turning over in her crib. Then the green eyes of that strange boy, the one who made the chain of my medal dig into my neck, the one who spit on me and breathed that awful smell from inside him, appeared in the darkness. His eyes watched me, then they closed, his face covered up with a white sheet.

"Pray for those who do not know the Lord."

It was the voice again and I was not afraid. I could hear a tune in my head like Joe hummed. It was low and full of sorrow, yet full of hope.

"Good night, my sweetie girls."

Mommy came in and kissed us. She smelled like coffee and cinnamon cake.

"Here's a little bite of cake, honey. Alice and I are not going anywhere tonight. We're getting ready for Easter, and we have too much baking to do. Now go to sleep."

I sat up in bed and ate the warm cake. The light from the bathroom came in and woke up Janey. I gave her a bite of cake and a sip of milk. Then I got up and turned off the light. There were no more eyes, no more voices, just the sound of Mommy and Alice baking Easter rolls.

Twenty-Five

White as Snow

Saturday was calm. Mommy and I cleaned the entire house that morning with ammonia and hot water. I used a broom to sweep all the cobwebs from the ceilings. I washed all the woodwork. Mommy scrubbed and waxed the wooden floors with lemon wax until they shined. Janey and I kept holding our heads over a shiny spot by the dining room window. The wax was so thick in one place that it made a mirror. We made faces at each other, and saw reflections in the floor. Janey crossed her eyes and opened her mouth so wide that you could see her teeth shine. It was like a picture of Janey's face was on the floor. Mommy gave us other jobs to do. I washed the wallpaper in the living room with pine oil soap. The roses became redder and the leaves appeared greener. Without any dirt, the background turned into a creamy color. I climbed onto a chair to wash the windows. Mommy had taken down all the curtains and washed them in the sink with baking soda and detergent, then soaked them in starch water and bluing. When they were dry, I ironed them. We hung them back up and they were lacy white, not gray anymore.

"Nobody had cleaned this place in sixty years, I bet!" Mommy told us.

"How old is this house, Mommy?" It was Janey.

"Sixty years, honey."

We all laughed. We were the first people to clean the house since it had been built. It had always been apartments, three stories with a wrap-around porch. One family moved out and left their dirt in the house. Then another family came in with their dirt to add to the rest. We lived in the front apartment on the right side, the largest. Nobody wanted to live in that one because the old woman who was there for fifteen years owned so many cats that the rooms smelled like cat pee. She'd passed away the year before, leaving her furniture. It was fancy black wood with carvings of fruit on the legs. Her bed and dining room set were the best. Mommy and I lifted the mattress up again the wall. She swept it then scrubbed it with boiling water and bleach. I helped her carry it outside on the porch so it could dry. The linoleum was worn away in the kitchen from so many tenants scuffing their feet through the years. Another reason that the landlord couldn't get anyone to take the apartment was because the old woman died there, but not in the bed. She fell in the bathroom and hit her head on the tub. A rumor had it that the place was haunted; in fact, the whole building was haunted according to neighbors. Mommy rented it since the landlord let us have it for only forty-five dollars a month. Mr. Barnett said he was tired of letting it go empty. A gigantic oil furnace in the basement heated all the rooms in the building. He agreed not to charge us for heat just to rent the place.

"Look at this fireplace!"

Mommy scooped all the ashes out and polished the mirror over the mantle. Her scarf was tied around her new hairdo to protect it. I thought that she looked prettier that day than I had ever seen her. She held baby Cissy up to the mirror so she could see herself. I watched them from the doorway where I was polishing all the brass doorknobs. We should keep cleaning and scrubbing forever, I thought. Trouble and bad things can't get into a house when it's clean. Cissy found her bottle and lay down on the shiny wooden floor. She stretched out, put her cheek down on the boards, and went to sleep. We tiptoed into the kitchen for lunch and left Cissy there, the air blowing our clean white curtains lightly over her. I turned my head back and I saw a robin come and perch on the windowsill, chirping and singing our baby to sleep.

"Mommy, will you let me go visit Polly now?"

I put the soup bowls in the sink and wrapped the cheese. We were finished cleaning our apartment, and I wanted to do something else.

"I guess. But just be back in time for dinner, before six."

Bernadette was in her store selling candy for Easter. I bought a handful of jellybeans from a glass jar. I gave her my dime and asked to see Polly.

"She is at the prayer service. This is Holy Saturday. You may go with me at 3:00 when I close."

I waited in the store until Bernadette was finished for the day. I walked up and down the aisles, straightening scarves, untangling necklaces. I lined up all the jars of cosmetics with the labels facing the front so the customers could read them better. I tried on every hat before I cleaned them with a feather duster, even the men's hats.

"Time to go now, Emmie."

I followed Bernadette down the street, out of our neighborhood. We walked down Pennsylvania Street, turned east on New Jersey until we came to a part of the city I was familiar with.

"Are we going to Sears?"

"No, little one. Put your eyes on the church across the street. The name is St. Mary's."

I found the Catholic Church after all. It was a huge building of white limestone and tall spires. Pigeons were everywhere, and they moved out of our way as we climbed the steps. I put my hand on the door handle, and a bell rang out clear and loud.

We pushed the huge, wooden doors open. Inside, it was cool and still. Only a few people were kneeling in the pews. I looked up to the domed ceiling where stained glass windows let in the light. There was a crucifix placed above the altar, a purple cloth covering the body of Jesus. I knelt down beside Bernadette. Polly and every one of her sisters were kneeling on the marble floor, making a line in front of the cross.

"Jesus is dead now on the cross. We put Him to death. Tomorrow, He will rise again. We wait with Him and His mother and the other women who waited by His tomb long ago."

I couldn't see the face of Jesus, but I knew that He was there. An old woman in the back of the church sang a hymn in a foreign language. There was no music, no piano playing, only the sound of her voice as she mourned our Lord.

"Jesus, Jesus, come again."

Bernadette spoke a little prayer after the woman's song was over. I saw her reach into her pocket and pull out a rosary. It was like the rosary I held when Polly was hurt. The clear beads made many colors as the light shined on them.

"This is the day of the glorious mystery as we wait for the coming of the Lord."

Bernadette said an introduction. The sisters led each decade of the rosary, and Polly said the Our Fathers. I had to say the "Glory Be."

"Glory be to our Father and to the Son and to the Holy Spirit—As it was in the beginning, is now and ever shall be. Amen."

The church inside became darker as the sun went down. All the candles burned down low, flickering, going out one by one. I knew that I had to get home, but I didn't want to leave Jesus alone. The priest walked up and down the aisles and talked to the few that remained.

"Go home now. Jesus will rise again on Easter morning."

Just then, the bell in the tower struck six times. I remembered what Mommy told me. I followed Bernadette and her daughters out of the church. The priest locked the doors behind us. Polly's sisters made clicking sounds with their shoes as we hurried down the steps. We made the sign of the cross before turning away. I stood at the corner, and the church was dark. No light came out of the windows, no women sang. Only the woman with a scarf covering her head knelt on the steps, her hands in prayer as she kept a vigil with the Lord. I walked home with Bernadette and her daughters that evening. There were dark gray clouds covering the sun. In the distance, the moon rose. There was darkness and light at the same time. We passed no one on the streets. Everyone must have been waiting for Jesus. At my house,

Bernadette thanked me for coming with her.

"There is nothing more important than keeping company with Jesus."

She pressed the crystal rosary into my hands and told me to keep it. The sisters gave me a kiss on the cheek and Polly hugged me.

"Happy Easter!"

Polly looked so healthy then. Her hair was shiny again, and her skin was clear. She had on a new blue blouse that she'd made herself. I went inside to continue my vigil. Mommy went to work and came home early that night. As soon as she kissed me good night, I fell asleep.

Twenty-Six

In the Name of Love

D addy came over early on Easter morning. I heard him knocking on the front window downstairs. I could see him standing there with his arms full of shopping bags looking up to see if we heard him.

"What do you have in those bags, Daddy?" I asked as I opened the door.

He came in and laid all the things on the dining room table. We pulled out slips, underwear, socks and hair ribbons. Mommy opened one bag.

"OOOH! Three yellow dresses for my girls."

Janey and Cissy got dressed right there in the dining room. They put on every new piece of clothing they could find. I took my dress and went into the bathroom to look at myself in the mirror. The dress had a satin collar and three buttons down the front. The full skirt fluffed out from my waist. I tied the belt in front and went out to show Mommy.

"All three of you match."

Daddy opened more boxes. He had a new pair of black patent leather shoes for each of us and a pair of nylons for me. Mommy had put on her navy blue suit and high heels while we were dressing. She had had it for years, but it was still nice. We waited out on the sidewalk, and Daddy combed Cissy's short hair with his pocket comb.

"Daddy, are these hats for us, too?"

Janey had found the bag with the white straw hats. They were all alike with thin yellow ribbons and tiny white flowers around the brims. There was one for each of us. He even gave Mommy a new lace veil for her head and a pair of white gloves. She dabbed a little bit of perfume on Janey and me and rubbed more rouge into her cheeks. Daddy was singing to Cissy out on the porch as he sat in the swing.

"Wake up Cissy baby, Cissy baby. We're going to church and then to the store."

Cissy danced up and down with her Easter hat on. Then Mommy locked the door and we started off down the street.

"Are we ready to go to church now, Daddy?"

Janey looked up and grabbed his hand. I walked behind them with Mommy by my side. We headed the same way that Bernadette went the day before. Daddy turned around to us.

"Look. I've found a Catholic church. Mass is starting now."

We followed him up the steps and inside. Daddy found a seat for us in the crowded church. I looked up at all the vases of white lilies in rows on the altar. A woman walked up the steps with a long stick. She had lit the end of it with one of the candles left burning from the vigil. Now there were tall candles standing upon the altar, resting in brass holders. She went from candle to candle and lit each one. They burned high and then flickered down into tiny flames. The purple cloth that was draped over the cross was gone. I sat beside Daddy and stared up at Jesus. The sun streamed down through the windows and lit up Jesus. His golden arms stretched out to the tips of the cross. A rusty nail drove down into each palm and His feet were stretched and bloody. I stared at the head as it hung down from the weight of death, the crown of thorns still embedded in His skull.

"What have people done to you, Jesus? Why can't you come down from your cross?"

I had many thoughts inside my head. The sun rose high over the church and the light came down to rest on my family and me. It only stayed with us a little while before it moved over to another row. I looked back and there was Bernadette and her daughters. Polly had on a pink and white shirt dress—American style. Her hair was twisted up on her head with a bow and she had a corsage of white roses. The light shined on her and her family, then bounced over to an old man who knelt on the cold floor. The light poured down on him hard. You could see the flecks of dust twirl around in the air and land on his collar. His suit turned from black to gray to white, the light was so strong on that old man. He must have felt me staring at him because he turned his head around and smiled. I could see his eyes clearly from a distance, bright and blue, and he nodded to me. He made the sign of the cross, and I copied him. Slowly the light moved away from the man and came to rest on Jesus. It stayed there for the rest of Mass.

"Why does the light only go to certain people?" I asked Jesus as He waited up there on the cross.

Then the choir began to sing, "Rise up, Rise up, all ye sinners. The light of Jesus comes to those who believe…"

After Mass was ended, the priest thanked us for coming and said his name was Father Philip.

"Keep the light of the risen Christ within your hearts. Now let us go out into the world and share that light with others."

At the door, I bumped into the old man who smiled at me during Mass.

"Don't lose your light, young lady."

Then he pressed a white lily into my hands. Daddy pinned the flower on my collar, and we walked back home for lunch. Mommy had put a ham into the oven to slow bake while we were at church. She and Alice had prepared macaroni salad and sliced tomatoes and cucumbers the night before. All we had to do was take everything out of the refrigerator and warm up the peas and pearl onions. I shaped the homemade dough into cloverleaf rolls, dropping three balls into greased muffin cups. Mommy and I had made the dough a few weeks before Easter and put it into the freezer. While we were at church, it thawed. I brushed the tops of the rolls with melted Crisco and put them into the oven to bake. We all sat down to a good lunch that day and nobody even noticed the mess Cissy made. Daddy brought a camera into the house. He took pictures of us eating and then washing dishes. Mommy set out a plate of coconut cookies and we stuffed ourselves. Daddy wanted us all to go walk around to digest our food.

"Let's go to the Monument and you can pose for me."

We drove over to the World War Memorial and parked the car on the street. Janey was the first to pose. She leaned up against the wall and put her hand on her waist like she was a movie star. We put Cissy on a ledge and taught her how to cross her legs. Mommy stood in front of the doors and wore her navy blue hat for the picture. There was a plaque on the wall.

FOR ALL THE BRAVE MEN AND WOMEN.

Janey stood beside it and pointed to the words. I took a picture of Daddy holding Cissy while they stood on the steps. I held the camera and stood down on the sidewalk below. In the picture, Daddy looked very tall, smiling and carrying the baby.

We walked all over downtown that Easter, stopping to pose in front of almost every building. In the park, a man was giving donkey rides. Daddy dropped some coins, and we waited our turn. We put Cissy on the front, then Janey. I rode on the back. The man walked us all over Memorial Park and around the block. His pointy hat said AMERICAN LEGION. Mommy waved at us as we passed her. Before we climbed down, Daddy took our picture on that donkey.

"Thank you for donating to poor Korean orphans" the man saluted us as we walked away.

"What are orphans? Where's Korea? What does donating mean?"

Janey was full of questions. She held my hand as I explained all the words to her.

"Orphans are kids who don't have any parents because they died in the war. And Korea is far away-near China where George used to live."

"Okay." Janey kept holding my hand.

"Then we are not orphans 'cause this is Indiana."

I wanted to explain more to her, but she kept getting confused.

"Orphans can live anywhere, Janey. Our mother and father don't live together. They're alive. And we are a little bit poor, but not like the children of Korea."

Janey let go of my hand and walked with Cissy to the car. She whispered something to Daddy, and I saw him put something in her hand. Together, they walked back over to the man with the donkey. I watched as Janey dropped more money into the collection bucket. When they reached us, she told me what she'd done.

"Maybe the poor orphans are hungry today. No one will give them anything to eat."

Daddy came in the house and had a ham sandwich and tea with us. When it was dark, we took Cissy's dress off her, changed her diaper and put on her gown. She kissed all of us goodnight. We waved to Daddy as he drove off in his car.

"Emmie, when is Daddy coming back?"

Janey waved and stared out the window.

"Next Saturday," I told her.

I looked out the window with her. It was dark and there were stars out. It was a good night, clear and cool. Janey said something else.

"The orphans will never have a Daddy to come and visit them, and it will always be dark at their house. And they won't have any ham and cookies and milk."

We went into the bedroom to go to sleep. I told her we had to say a prayer.

"Dear God. Please send food to the orphans of Korea, and please bring our Daddy back again next week. Thank you."

Twenty-Seven

In God's Country

❧

We were back in school on Monday after Easter. Mr. Ramsey asked the students to write an essay of what we did during our time off. One girl wrote a very funny description about coloring eggs and another boy described riding the bus to Chicago to visit relatives. Joe got up in front of the class and told us how he practiced singing every day, getting ready for the Easter morning service. His descriptions of the songs made me hear them in my mind.

"Would you like me to sing for the class, Mr. Ramsey?"

"Uh…not now, Joe. We don't have enough time. George, get up and read your essay to the class."

George rose from his desk and walked to the front of the classroom. He stood beside Mr. Ramsey's desk, so short yet he held his head up so high.

"Mmmmm…"

George cleared his throat, coughed, and swallowed before he began.

"My family go, ahh, went to downtown. We become citizens of United States. Thank you. I am American now. I keep going to school and study English."

"Very good, George! It's a little short. Next time try to write more paragraphs. Congratulations."

Mr. Ramsey shook hands with George before he went back to his desk. Polly got up in of the class and read her essay about sewing. She made pillows and then embroidered birds and flowers on them.

"My mother sold all the pillows. She sent the money to my father in Romania. He is coming here this year."

Polly smiled so wide when she finished reading. I got out of my seat to stand beside Mr. Ramsey and I began to read my paper.

"I went to the Catholic church."

All the students stared at me wide-eyed.

"There are many churches in Indianapolis, but I love St. Mary's best of all. Jesus is there on the cross, waiting to come down and save us all. The Catholic Church is open to everyone. Go inside and look at the flowers and the statues and the light."

"Emmie, how different your essay is from the others. Yet, still, it is interesting. Now I'll grade your spelling and penmanship with the rest."

I placed my sheet of notebook paper on top of the stack face up. There at the top of the page, I had written the letters JMJ just like the nuns taught me in kindergarten.

"Come back, Emmie. What do these letters mean?"

He held out my paper and pointed to the top.

"They mean Jesus, Mary and Joseph. The Holy Family. I dedicated my writing to them."

"Oh, I see."

Mr. Ramsey looked startled for a second but then he smiled.

"Sit down now, Emmie."

There we were in the front row, Joe, George, Polly and I. Mr. Ramsey put our stack of essays in his briefcase to grade at home. I turned around just a little. The other students all seemed nice and friendly, but I didn't have strong feelings for them. A few did not really like school. They seemed to be without something that my friends had. Joe had so much love when he sang, and George was very patriotic. Polly knew many religious things, and she was devoted to God. But what did I have? I had many thoughts about people and things and a need to find out why evil happened in the world. The other kids went home to watch cartoons and maybe do their homework. We were different, the four of us, and I didn't know why. Even Janey was different from the other kids her age. She could ask questions and really make me think hard. Other kids didn't want to know anything like Janey did.

"Pay attention, Emmie! I asked you to read chapter twelve in your history book."

I fumbled with the pages, finally coming to the picture of the Statue of Liberty.

"By the middle of the 1800s, many people were coming to our shores…"

George sat up straight and listened to me read, his hands folded almost in prayer.

"Facing poverty, starvation, persecution and political troubles, immigrants of every race and from all countries of the earth saw America as a beacon of hope."

George shook his head up and down as if he was saying yes. In our book, there was a picture of different races of people gathered at the foot of the Statue of Liberty. They were waiting in line to become Americans. The first family in line had a group of little red-haired children. The caption under the photograph caught my eye.

The O'Brien family waits to enter the United States.

O'Brien. O'Brien. O'Brien. I read that silently to myself while still staring at my book.

"Now everyone take out a sheet of paper. Answer the eight questions at the end of your chapter. We have thirty minutes before the bell."

Mr. Ramsey stood by the door and pointed to the clock. I thought about the first question that asked why people wanted to come to this country. George was tapping me on the shoulder.

"How do you spell persecution?"

I whispered how to spell the word and watched as George wrote furiously. His answer contained something that made him very angry and serious. His pencil made scraping sounds on the paper, he was writing so fast. Everyone heard when it snapped in two and rolled in pieces to the floor. Mr. Ramsey walked over to hand George another one. I leaned over and read George's answer.

"People came to America because here you can write anything and think your own thoughts even if they are different from others. You can say things without going to jail or being killed."

I watched the clock hands move slowly toward 3:00. All the kids were writing fast but George and Joe were done. Polly smiled when she finished. The bell rang, and I just barely made it. I wrote an entire page on why immigration was a good thing for the United States. My friends waited for me outside the classroom door.

"What took you so long, Emmie?"

Joe wanted to get home and practice the piano.

"I was writing about immigration and I couldn't stop. We are all immigrants when you think about it."

A boy from another seventh-grade class overheard me say that.

"You're all weird. That's what you are. Weirdos! None of you are true Americans."

He laughed then and walked past us, bumping into George on purpose. The mean boy laughed all the way out of the building.

"Weirdos, Weirdos, Immigrant Weirdos!"

It was hard to leave school that day. We had been encouraged to think and write. But we walked past that boy as he hung around the front door. He followed us home the entire way down Central, yelling and laughing until we reached Joe's house. His mama came out on the porch.

"Go away, you heathen! Give some respect for our brothers and sisters!"

The boy kept walking. He didn't say anything else, just kept laughing until we couldn't hear him anymore.

"Children, forgive the ignorant. Call on the Lord in your time of need."

We had a snack at Joe's house of toast and peanut butter. We didn't stay long since Joe had a piano lesson at four. I walked George and Polly to their houses.

"See you tomorrow" Polly assured me.

George waved as he walked up to his steps.

Someone had hung the American flag from a pole in the front yard. It waved back and forth in the afternoon breeze as George yelled out to the street.

"I am American. I am American!"

His grandma came and opened the front door. She leaned over to whisper something in his ear. Then George yelled out again. He climbed up on the porch ledge and held up his arms.

"Grandma American too!"

Janey and I laughed, and then she started yelling.

"I'm American!"

Now it was my turn.

"I'm American!"

George yelled out one more time into the street.

"We are all American!"

I waved goodbye.

"See you tomorrow on the corner, George."

He and Grandma bowed to us. The last thing I saw was when they saluted the flag flying high over their house. We could hear the flapping sound of the cloth hitting the pole as Janey and I hurried home that day.

Twenty-Eight

Amazing Grace

M y back was cold when I woke up the next morning. I wasn't even sure what time it was but I knew we had to get up for school. I changed Cissy's diaper before I put her down in the crib. She grabbed the bottle and made a funny face when she learned it was only water. I left her there in bed and pulled the covers up.

"Be a good girl while Mommy's sleeping. I'll bring you some milk after school."

Mommy was lying in bed, her outstretched hand holding a cigarette. The fire had burned out and only ashes remained on the tip. When I took it out of her fingers, she rolled over away from me. I wanted to stay home with her and the baby, but I couldn't. My teacher would get mad at me if I was absent and someone had to walk Janey to school. I grabbed Janey's hand and we started down the steps. She did not have any socks on. We would be late if I hunted for a pair and I knew we didn't have clean ones anyway.

"Sit down and put my socks on. Here."

I would pretend that I had silk hose on if anyone said something to me. I noticed Janey's hair with the frizzy, curly knots.

"Hurry, Janey. Walk faster."

I grabbed her and ran my fingers through her hair, trying to remove some of the knots as we walked. She looked like she had never combed her hair in her life.

"What about breakfast Emmie?"

Janey looked up at me with her blue eyes before she went into her classroom.

"We'll eat at lunchtime Janey. Just wait" I promised her.

I could see the back of her hem coming undone on the dress. It had been like that yesterday, but Mommy didn't fix it. I hoped nobody made fun of her dress and her tangled hair. I was thinking of so many things as I walked into my own classroom. All the kids were in their seats. I heard the bell ring while I took Janey to her class. As I crossed in front of Mr. Ramsey, I held my head down, hoping he would not notice that I wasn't wearing any socks. At lunchtime, he called me up to his desk.

"Is anything wrong Emmie?"

"No! It was hot today, so I don't have any socks."

He gave me a strange look, but then told me to go to lunch.

"Fine. Let me know if you need something."

Janey was waiting by her classroom door for me. We walked slowly behind the other kids who were going home for lunch. I knew Mommy was still sick and there was no food in the house. On the corner of 22nd Street and Central, there was a drugstore. The owner was a pharmacist who also ran a lunch counter. We walked in and saw the row of stools empty except for two customers. Both men ate bacon and tomato sandwiches. The smell of the bacon was smoky and sweet as we stood nearby. I picked up a magazine from the rack and looked at the ads for lipstick. The models all had such white teeth and beautiful smiles. I stretched my lips wide and pretended that I was a model in Hollywood. I also read a recipe for Spanish Chicken and Rice. Janey sat on the floor looking at comic books. We saw the hot dogs turn around and around in the electric warmer, their edges getting brown and crispy. When the juice from the hot dogs hit the heat, they made a sizzling sound. Janey looked up at the hot dog machine. I could see her frowning with that look of hers. I kept thinking that I didn't have any money in my pocket. Then the man said he was going to throw the hot dogs away because they were old.

"You want these hot dogs? Here, sit up on the stool."

"I don't have any money today."

"Never mind."

He helped Janey step up when he noticed she couldn't reach the stool. He gave her a glass of chocolate milk and she drank it right away. When Mr. Farmer sat the plates in front of us, there was Coney sauce on top of the hot dogs. His wife placed little bowls of coleslaw and peaches next to them. She even gave us each a handful of potato chips. I drank my ginger ale down and she refilled my glass. We were almost finished when Mrs. Farmer slid a piece of pumpkin pie toward Janey and me. I could see the kids pass by the window going back to class. We hurried to finish all our food. At the door, I turned around and waved at Mr. Farmer.

"Thank you. That was delicious!"

He nodded his head as he wiped off the counter. We heard him whistling when we closed the door. Janey and I walked fast on our way back to school, even running some. When the bell rang at 3:00, Janey reminded me about Cissy.

"She's probably really hungry now."

I had a good idea of what to do.

Twenty-Nine

Lonely Teardrops

W e made our way to the meat market by our house. I walked up to Mr. Steinbaum and asked if we could open a charge account. "What is your last name, Emmie?"

"O'Brien."

"And when can you pay?"

"Umm…next month…I think."

He squinted his eyes together as if he was thinking of something very important and then handed me a small wire basket across the counter.

"You may fill this up, young lady."

I carried the basket around the store and chose our items with a lot of care. For Cissy, I put in a box of baby rice cereal and a few jars of bananas. I saw a can of powdered milk with a baby's face that looked just like my baby sister, so I got that also. Janey went from aisle to aisle and returned with a can of peas, some potatoes and a box of butterscotch pudding mix. She tugged on my dress and pointed to the soap aisle. We dropped a roll of toilet tissue and bar of Ivory soap in the basket. The basket was getting pretty heavy after we'd added bread, butter and a quart of milk. I walked up to the meat counter and ordered the final thing.

"We will have four of those cubed steaks, please."

I told him we had enough food, so Mr. Steinbaum rang up all the items on his adding machine. The white tab kept rolling out of the machine with every price. I was afraid. I didn't think we were stealing, but something wasn't right. He didn't ring up our order on the cash register.

"That will be $12.40. Sign here. Put your address and the date also."

After I signed the book, he snapped it shut and began to place all the food in a paper sack. He winked at Janey and me, and then grabbed a handful of gumballs and two bags of peanuts. Janey could not believe it when she saw the candy and nuts go down into the bag. I was surprised when he put a bottle of orange juice, some eggs and apples in it."

Looks like you need two sacks girlies! Want to use my personal cart?"

I said yes, so he loaded the cart and pushed open the front door.

"You can put my cart by the back door in the alley later. Come back again Monday. Round steak will be on sale. So delicious with mushroom gravy."

Mommy was drinking again when Janey and I walked in with the groceries.

"Where did you get all that?"

Her hair was still tangled up on top of her head. The gown was gone, and she wore a sleeveless pink blouse and stretch pants. I was a bit afraid to tell her about signing the book.

"I opened up a charge account with the butcher. He's really nice and we can pay him next month."

I could tell she wasn't mad at me.

"Some friends from work are coming over tonight."

I went to get Cissy. She had been in bed most of the day. I cleaned her up, pinning a dishtowel on her bottom for a diaper and carried her into the living room.

"Watch Cissy while I cook supper."

Janey wrapped the baby up in a blanket while they watched cartoons. I went back to the kitchen to put the groceries away. I had watched Mommy cook cubed steak before, so I knew how to do it. Dust with flour and sprinkle salt and pepper, and then fry them in hot grease. It was fun and not too difficult. I boiled four potatoes and warmed the peas. While supper was getting done,

I cooked the pudding for Janey and Cissy. Mommy had a pink china bowl on the top shelf but I couldn't reach it. She got up from her chair and got the bowl for me, almost falling into the stove. I helped her back to her seat and emptied the ashtray once again.

"Thanks for cooking, Honey."

Her words were funny, not right. They sounded like she was talking with something in her mouth. Where did she get another bottle of vodka and more soda pop? I knew the tavern was two blocks away. I thought she didn't have any money and when I left for school, she was in a deep sleep. If she'd walked there, that meant she left Cissy alone. Or maybe she carried her. Finally, the food was ready. Janey and Cissy sat down at the table. Cissy could barely reach the table, she was so little. I got the phone book and placed her on top of it, then pushed her up to the table. She was right next to Janey so she could catch Cissy if she began to fall. Mommy didn't want anything to eat. She smoked while we ate and mixed herself another drink. I cut up Cissy's steak in tiny pieces. She liked it when I mashed her potatoes together with the peas and a pat of butter on top. The plate sat untouched in front of Mommy while she smoked more. At last, she ate half the meat and a piece of bread. Janey ate the rest of Mommy's supper. It was so quiet there in the kitchen that night. All we could hear was the ticking of the clock. I jumped when the window rattled. It was cold and dark that night.

We were finished eating when the doorbell rang. I opened it and let in Mommy's group of friends. They were noisy, bouncing Cissy up and down so much that I was afraid they'd make her throw up. One of the women lit a cigarette and blew the smoke in my face. The tall guy with the curly blond hair was sort of handsome, but he was very drunk. I had met him before at the tavern where he used to play with his band. He smoked some small cigars that stunk so bad, I got dizzy. He had on jeans and a black leather vest with his silk shirtsleeves rolled up to his elbows. When he sat down, he crossed his legs and I noticed the boots. They were pointy and made out of snakeskin with buckles on the side. I could see a knife stuck down through the side of his right boot. All I could see was the handle and an inch of the silver blade. He caught me staring at his knife and winked at me, pulling it out of his boot.

"This here is in case anyone gives me trouble. You don't want any bad men to hurt old Sonny and your Momma, do you?"

That knife was about ten inches long and looked so sharp. He stroked it on the bottom of his heel where there were metal plates and then put the knife back into its resting place. If his pants leg was pulled down over the boot, you couldn't notice the knife. I was still staring at him when he opened his vest. There were pockets inside full of everything. He had a lighter and a can of lighter fluid and a pack of cigars. On the other side, he had a leather flask. He opened the top of the flask and tipped it up to his mouth for a long time.

"Want a swig of moonshine, Cutie?"

"Me? I don't drink. I'm too young."

"Was just testin' ya darlin'. Bottle of this, and your brains'll be fried. Won't know here from heaven. Or the other place. Say, why don't you get ole Sonny some ice now, sweet thing?"

The other men were drinking, but they weren't like Sonny. One of them gave me a look like he was mad at me, so I turned my head. He seemed like he thought everything was so funny. He kept laughing at whatever anyone said even if it wasn't funny. I saw him reach into his pocket and take out two shiny black capsules. He offered one to Sonny, but Sonny said no, so he swallowed both pills without any water. The two women had on white blouses but they were dirty, as if they had worn the same clothes for a week. One of the women had long black hair, straight down to her rear end. She sat on the lap of the man who swallowed the pills. She leaned backward and blew smoke rings in the air. The laughing man thought that was funny. The other woman was fat. Her skirt was too short and you could see her fat knees. I thought that if her skirt was a little longer and she would take a bath, she would be the nicest one. She didn't talk much and once she winked at me. I did like her hairdo. It was curly, shiny red and she had such pretty blue eyes. She didn't smoke like everyone else. Her drink sat in front of her for a long time and she only sipped from it a few times.

I stayed in the kitchen long enough to form an opinion of the people. When they began singing along with the radio and screaming, I left. I grabbed the bowl of pudding and a couple of spoons and headed for the living room. The visitors and Mommy laughed at silly jokes that I couldn't understand. Sometimes they yelled like strange animals. Sonny brought along his guitar to play. He was a good singer, and I liked his songs. But the other people would not be quiet long enough for him to finish. My sisters and I were in the other room, but we could hear every word. One of the couples went out to buy more liquor and cigarettes. I heard them on the front porch before they knocked.

"Got me a Wild Turkey and our friend Jim Beam. Old Jack Daniels loves me the most."

They made stupid jokes about the names on the bottles. The woman with the long Indian-style hair came into the living room and pinched Janey's cheek. Janey didn't say anything. She kept her eyes glued to the television. We were watching Lawrence Welk and Janey did not want to miss the polka dancers. I prayed real hard that the woman wouldn't come over and pinch my cheek or bother Cissy. The woman stood and watched us for a minute, then left the room. She was muttering about how boring we were.

Suddenly, I remembered about Cissy's diapers. They were hard to wash. I dipped them all in the toilet and squeezed the stinky water out by hand. I fixed a tub of soapy water with Spic and Span and dumped the diapers in. Then I spotted a back brush with a long handle. I used that to stir the diapers around in the suds. We had plastic curtains in the bathroom, the kind that landlords always hung up that came from the dime store. The curtains were so cheap that they were almost see-through. I began to stare at the flower-design. Some of the flowers seemed as if they had faces and they were watching me. I saw eyes everywhere even in the tub. I was feeling dizzy and hot even though I was only wearing a towel. I thought I heard the eyes telling me to get in the water. It was so humid that the mirror fogged up. I began gasping and choking so I opened the door. Janey must have heard me because she asked me if I was sick. She looked so serious. Her face was getting pink from the heat. The window was open and a breeze blew open the curtains. The room was normal now and I felt better. I made Janey take off her dress and put on a sweater of Daddy's he left at the house one day.

"Take everything off, Janey, and put it in the tub."

I gathered all the dirty clothes I could find, our blue plaid jumpers, blouses and underwear. Mommy's gown, bras, our slips, socks, and Cissy's baby clothes went into the tub. There I stood, naked, wrapped up in an old towel, washing our clothes by hand. When they had soaked for a while, I drained the suds water and added a few drops of Mommy's perfume to the rinse water. There were clothes everywhere. I wrung each piece as dry as possible and used all the furniture for clotheslines. I hung clothes on the sofa, the living room chairs, even Cissy's crib had clothes draped over it, soaking her mattress and the rug. I draped two sheets over the wooden porch railing outside even though it was cold. I could hear those people talking and singing in the kitchen. Mommy came in the bathroom then.

"We're going to hear the band play. Put some clothes on, Emmie. Do you hear?"

She could barely stand up. Mommy leaned against the bathroom door while she applied blue eye shadow on her lids. With a long comb, she ratted her hair, piling it up on her head with bobby pins. When her hair was all high, she gave it a heavy spray with Aqua Net. I knew you couldn't smoke while you sprayed it because I had read the can many times. Mommy smoked the whole time in the bathroom, and I was afraid of an explosion.

"I'm leaving now. Lock the door."

I watched her go away. She was weaving, not walking straight down the hall. Her high-heeled go-go boots made her look too tall. I hated those things.

Thirty

Turn the Page

T he kitchen was a mess after all the people left. I brought the trashcan over to the table and swept the ashes into it with my hand. The different colored bottles broke when I smashed them with the skillet. The pieces were sparkly, but the edges were sharp. I used the broom to sweep them up. Some of the pieces were tiny, and they stuck to the linoleum, shining when the light hit them. Someone had left a pill on the table-one of the black ones. I opened the capsule, and a bunch of tiny yellow balls spilled on the tablecloth. They rolled under the chairs and toward the back door. What if Cissy ate them? She liked to eat things off the floor. I just kept sweeping and sweeping, pushing the bad things out onto the back step. I mopped next with hot water and dish detergent, so hot I could barely wring out the mop. The wind was cold that night. I thought I saw someone out in the back alley looking at me, and I ran back into the house. I was sweaty from the heat and the cold and trying to remove the tiny sparkly pieces of glass and pills on the floor.

"Where is Cissy's gown?"

It was Janey standing next to me. I hadn't heard her come into the kitchen.

I told her to go get the gown from the bathroom towel rack.

"It's still wet. Can you dry it for her?"

I turned on the oven to 350 degrees and opened the door. I hung the gown and a few other things over a chair in front of the oven. We kept touching the clothes to see if they were dry, but we had to do this many times. She and I sat together on another chair in front of the open oven door waiting. It was late that night when Janey and I took our baths and put on clean underwear. We dressed Cissy so she could go back to bed. We left all the lights on in the house until Mommy came home. But she never came back that night.

Janey and I didn't go to school the rest of the week. I designed some crossword puzzles on a piece of cardboard I found in the alley. When I finished that, I helped Janey draw paper dolls on a brown paper grocery sack. The television played Afternoon at the Movies each day at four. We played checkers on a used set that Alice gave us, and I read some pages in Mommy's bible. Proverbs 1:33 was my favorite. *For whoever listens to me will live in safety, and be at ease without fear of harm.* I liked the part about safety.

"Emmie, I will listen to God."

I cooked toast and honey butter and I boiled some rice with salt and pepper. Mr. Steinbaum let us charge a pound of ham, soup, baby formula, bread and milk.

"Take these oranges, Emmie. And some tea. You like tea, don't you? Here's a half-pound of sugar and a stick of oleo."

Janey and I had pushed Cissy to the market in the metal shopping cart. Mr. Steinbaum let us keep it at our house. I made sure to go down the alley so none of the kids from school would see. Mommy came home on Friday night and said she had been in jail.

"But I didn't do anything. Some people were fighting and the police took everybody away. They wouldn't let me call your Daddy at work."

I started thinking hard. Did any of my friends or the kids at school have mothers who went to jail? I hoped they did not learn about Mommy. She finally came home and we were so happy. On the way home from jail, she had stopped at the market. Mommy cooked that night. She made biscuits and gravy with eggs. I ate five biscuits. My stomach felt so heavy, but I was not sick.

"Where is Janey's dress? I have to sew the hem. And go do your homework. Cissy can play on the dining room floor. We'll go in there."

I didn't have any homework because I'd finished it three days before, the last day we went to school. We took Mommy her sewing basket. Cissy clapped her hands while she rolled a little toy car across the floor. Janey sat next to Mommy's feet and laughed at a funny story in her reading book. I got out my pad of paper to write an essay about a subject in our health book. I wrote three pages about the dangers of drinking alcohol and the effect on the human body. For my essay, I created a character of an old man who sat in his kitchen at night, not bathing or eating, just staring at the clock. He was a sick old man and I felt sorry for him. But as I wrote, I began to feel angry. If only he could see what he was doing to his family. They would not even visit him, they were so upset. Some neighbors found the old man dead. The alcohol had rotted his brain and killed him. At the end of the story, he was slumped over the table, an empty bottle of vodka clutched tightly in his hands. Mr. Ramsey graded our essays the next week and handed them back. At the top of mine, he had written a few comments.

"You really understand the health risks of alcohol. Your story is very imaginative. Where do you get your inspiration? A+"

That night, Mommy cooked fried chicken with mashed potatoes and gravy for our dinner. I told her that I received an A+ on my health essay, but I wouldn't let her read it. She told us stories about growing up in Tennessee. The radio played happy songs that night.

Thirty-One

What Child is This?

W e were awake early the first Saturday in May. Mommy was in the kitchen rolling out pie crusts with her wooden pin. I watched her stretch the dough out in a circle that covered the table. She took a knife and cut out four circles to fit the metal pans.

"Mommy! Can I pour in the filling?"

She let me add the mixture of raspberries thickened with lots of sugar and cornstarch. The day before, the Vegetable Man, had come around. That's what everyone called him, but I knew his name was really Paul because I'd heard his wife calling him that. He drove slowly up and down the streets, calling out what he had for sale.

"Fressssshhhh raspberries straight from the farm. Carrots, onions, cabbage, chives. I got green beans galore."

We bought green beans, tomatoes and two quarts of the raspberries. Mommy cut out long strips of crust to make a crisscross pattern on top of the pies. Next, she brushed the tops with melted butter and sprinkled sugar. As she opened the oven door, I heard voices out on the porch. When I opened the door, I saw Polly.

"Will you come out, Emmie? We don't know what to do. No school!"

I had a perfect idea.

"Let's go look at buildings. That's always fun."

We walked over to George's house. He was sitting on the front steps shining his father's shoes.

"We are going on a tour, George. Do you want to go along?"

Mr. Washington took the shoes and supplies from George and waved him away. We then went to Joe's house. His mother opened the door.

"What do you want Precious?"

"My friends and I are going on a tour of buildings. Will you let Joe go with us?"

"My goodness, yes. Of course, you will come back in time for his lunch, won't you?"

"Oh yeah! We'll be back in time."

Joe brought along his sketchpad and pencils. We stopped in front of some houses so that Joe could draw them. He made each different than they really were. On one porch, he drew a little girl wearing a pretty white dress. There was really a little girl on the porch of the house, but her dress was old and gray. In the drawing, she had red bows on her pigtails, but in real life, her hair was greasy and uncombed. The girl looked down at us from her porch, and she had such a lonely look in her eyes. Joe made her smile in the drawing. He added birds that sat all around her.

"Joe's an artist. Want to see what he drew?"

I called out to the little girl on the porch to come and join us. As she walked toward us, I could see that she had scratches on her arms. One of her eyes had a dark circle around it. Green and purple spots were on her neck. And the buckle straps on her shoes were broken. Joe held the sketchpad so the girl could see herself as he saw her. Her eyes were bright blue in the picture. I looked at her and as the tears came to her eyes, they changed from gray to blue. The morning light shined behind her so brightly that for a minute, her dress really was white and her greasy hair seemed shiny and yellow. A little robin redbreast came and landed by her feet. The light was almost blinding me that I had to look down. That's when I saw that her shoes were no longer dusty and worn out. They shined on her like new patent leather.

"What is your name?" Joe asked her.

"I am Mary."

Joe wrote Mary's name and drew a big yellow sun behind her head in the drawing. He tore off the sheet from his book and gave it to the little girl. She reached out to grab the picture, staring at it with bright eyes, but only for a few seconds. She turned around away from us.

"Thank you. It's truly beautiful."

"Wait! Where are you from Mary?"

I wanted to know what place she'd come from.

"I'm not from here. I'm from Kentucky, but I live in many houses. I move a lot because my Paw gets drunk, and he loses all our money. Sometimes people make us leave. My little brother and I don't know anybody in this town."

Then a cute little boy about two years old appeared by the side of the porch. He didn't have any pants on, only a dirty diaper held on with rusty pins. His hair was blond like Mary's and he had the same eyes.

"Can you go on a tour with us, Mary?"

She seemed surprised when I asked her to come with us, but she folded up Joe's drawing and stuffed it into the pocket of her dress.

"Only if my baby brother Dewey can come too. I'm watching him while Ma and Paw work."

She grabbed Dewey's hand, and he walked beside her as Mary joined our group. We traveled all over the neighborhood from 22nd Street, over to Park, down to 16th Street and over to North Meridian. We went past the Indianapolis Public Library and over to the Murat Temple. Joe drew the buildings while we waited. Polly took baby Dewey in her arms. He was fascinated with her earrings and necklaces. He got under her long skirt and peeked out at us. I told Mary all about Indianapolis. Each building had a meaning, each street had a name. She wanted to know where we came from.

"I am from Romania," said Polly.

"From Alabama" Joe called out.

"I am from China but now American." George held his hand over his heart

137

when he spoke.

"And I'm from the Eastside of Indianapolis. I'm a Hoosier," I told Mary.

She stood on the sidewalk there at New York and East Street looking at all the buildings. The German Club was having a party at the Athenaeum, their accordion music drifting out the windows toward us. The Shriners with their red hats came out of the Murat to the parking lot to practice riding those tricycles for the Indianapolis 500 Parade. A tall black man wearing a shirt of many colors, colors like Polly's skirt, passed by. The huge necklace he wore looked like a rosary with white wood beads the size of golf balls. We stopped to look at him, and he smiled at us.

"Peace, children. Love to all!"

Mary looked toward Monument Circle.

"Who is that lady on the monument? I see her everywhere."

I had to tell her.

"That is Lady Victory. She watches over our city so enemies do not overtake it."

A beggar man came to us then and told me that another man was watching us.

"He steals little children. Get out of his way. Do not look at him, and do not talk to him. Leave now and hurry on your way."

From the corner of my eye, all I could see was someone in gray clothes. I grabbed Mary's hand, Polly scooped up Dewey and everyone followed me. I heard bells then, so we went to see where they were coming from. We stood in front of Saint Mary's Church where I had gone with Polly and her mother and where my family went to Mass for Easter. A bride and groom came out, and all the people threw rice at the newlyweds. One of the bridesmaids gave us each small bags of candy mints tied with yellow ribbons.

"What a nice city this is. Even the beggars protect you from bad men and now gifts from people I don't even know."

Mary ran into the church with her mouth open, her eyes gazing at all the saints. We went up to the place where the Virgin Mary was standing. There was a basket of white roses at her feet. A nun wearing her long black habit came up to us.

"Hello! My name is Sister Felicia. Would you children like to crown our Holy Mother today?" Then she handed Mary the crown of flowers.

"Step up and honor her on this day."

The sister led Mary by the hand and guided her toward the statue. Mary climbed the marble steps where the nun had placed a wooden step stool. Mary was tall enough then, and she reached up to place the crown on the statue's head. The Lady in the blue dress held her hands out to the little girl in the dirty gray dress, the one who had a black eye and bruises and scrapes. But I knew there was another girl inside the one we saw. That girl was happy, dressed in white with red bows in her shiny yellow hair. The other girl inside of Mary was the one she carried in the pocket of her dress. She was the same one that Joe had seen with his artist's eyes-the girl he made us see.

We ran up to the altar to be with Mary. Our Lady looked down at us children kneeling on the cold marble floor. I held baby Dewey in my arms. He had reached for me, and I took him. He had no shirt on, so I wrapped him up in my arms. Polly spread her shawl over him. He fell asleep with his face buried in my neck. Sister Felicia knelt beside us and said that we were honoring the mother of Jesus.

"He became human, and He needed a mother to take care of Him."

The bells struck again, so we got up to leave.

Sister followed us as we went outside. "Jesus is always here for you."

She beat her fist hard on her chest.

"Ask Mary, His mother, to care for you just as she cares for the son of God."

We looked again at the church. The spires reached up high. A dove sang out. It flew down and dropped a white rose on the sidewalk in front of Mary.

"I have never been inside a church before."

Mary talked about Saint Mary's church as we walked.

"Is it open every day? Can anyone go? What do you need to get in?"

When we reached her house, her father was waiting. He came down the stairs and yanked her arm, pulling and dragging her and Dewey into the house. Dewey tripped on the broken porch step and fell on his knee. I called to her.

"Don't forget about Jesus and His mother!"

When her father heard that, he slammed the door and broke the glass. Mary's mother ran out and picked up Joe's drawing that had fallen out of Mary's pocket. She unfolded it, and her eyes lit up when she saw what it was. Then she folded it and threw the paper on the ground.

"Here. You keep it. Mary's Paw won't let her have anything like that."

George was fast. He snatched up the paper, and we ran. Mary's Paw came after us, but he was drunk and got out of breath real fast. His large, fat face turned red, he was so full of hate.

"You kids get outta here. Don't be fillin' my girl's head full of that religious crap. Come around again and I'll beat you with my belt."

We hurried to Joe's house. Mrs. Dorster hugged us when we sat down to lunch. She ladled potato soup into our bowls. I wondered if Mary would have any lunch that day. I would ask her to come here to this warm kitchen. Joe's mama would love to have another mouth to feed.

Thirty-Two

That's What Friends Are For

T here was only about a month before school let out for the summer. My friends and I walked slowly on that Monday morning. It was sunny and warm, so all the lilac bushes were blooming. We stopped to admire a fence blanketed with purple morning glories. A hummingbird hovered over the fence. I heard footsteps behind me, but they stopped all the sudden. The new girl, Mary, waited on the sidewalk until we took off walking. I wanted her to join us and I called out to her.

"Mary! Over here, Mary!"

She stopped and looked at the ground as if she were searching for something that was lost. I got the feeling that she wanted to be with us, yet she kept still. Her mother came out and whispered something in her ear, and then Mary walked slowly behind us. It was like that all the way to school. Mary stayed a few feet behind as she followed us into the school building. From my desk, I could see her hanging around the classroom door. Mr. Ramsey must have noticed her finally because he went out into the hallway. I could see Mary nodding her head every time she was asked a question.

There was an empty seat behind me. The little girl who had it all year long had just moved away with her dad to Germany. He was in the army and took the family. Mr. Ramsey guided Mary.

"Sit behind Emmie. She can give you all the help you need."

I turned around and said something quietly to her.

"Hi Mary. Glad you're in our class."

She started to smile, but her mouth had a little dried blood in the corner. It was as if her lips were frozen shut into a straight line. She had on a light tan dress with little white flowers. It would have been a pretty outfit if she did not have grease stains all down the front of it and if her mother would have sewn the collar where it was ripped. Maybe I'd ask her to come home with me. I'd invent some excuse to get her to change her clothes. We could play dress up in Mommy's waitress uniform. Then while she wasn't looking, I'd scrub those stains out of her dress. I could make a paste of detergent and soak the dress in warm water and baking soda. Tomorrow, she'd be dressed better. She would be clean.

"Emmie, please pass out one of these symbols to each student."

It was Mr. Ramsey again, shaking me awake out of my thoughts and into the classroom. They were little cardboard cutouts of American cities. There was the Statue of Liberty for New York, the White House for Washington, D.C. and a plate of barbecued ribs for Kansas City. Each student had to identify what city their symbol represented. We had to write a brief report of what we knew about that city. George was lucky. He picked our nation's Capital out of the box when I came to his desk. His pen scratched the paper as he wrote furiously about his favorite place. I saw Polly daydreaming then she showed me her symbol of the Golden Gate Bridge in San Francisco. Joe was turning his cutout of Miami in his hands. It had a picture of a large hotel on the beach with palm trees and Cuban dancers. I had the symbol for Philadelphia, the Liberty Bell. I wrote a page on the Declaration of Independence. When I finished and the class was still writing, I turned around. There on Mary's desk was the symbol of Indianapolis— Monument Circle with the Lady Victory on top waving her sword and a race car going around an oval. There was a man waving a black and white checkered flag and blowing a whistle.

"Mary, get up and read your paper."

Mr. Ramsey smiled at the new girl. I turned in my seat while she stood up.

"There are many beautiful things about Indianapolis-museums with art and churches that are full of God. We have neighborhoods with different kinds of houses. But the most beautiful thing is the children who are nice and friendly and help me every day."

Mr. Ramsey clapped his hands. "Welcome to Indianapolis Mary."

We all clapped our hands before Mary sat down. She had little tears on her face, and her mouth was beginning to open. Before I turned around to do my math problems, I noticed her lips moving. She was making silent words. It looked like she made the words "Thank you, Jesus."

I had a new friend. She and I would walk home with the group, and I would give her a barrette for her hair. We could play beautician. I would pin up her hair and put some beauty cream on Mary's face to get rid of the dried scabs. Then I would put ice packs on her purple bruises. Maybe we had some ointment to put on her scratches and then they would heal. I would ask Mommy if I could use some of her curlers to roll Mary's hair. While her hair set, we could read magazines and talk about movie stars. And when she was all cleaned up on the outside, we'd go to the Circle, climb all the way up the steps and look out over Indianapolis. Mary only stayed three weeks in our city. Her father got mad because he knew we liked her and she talked to our group. One day, he was waiting for her after school. Their car was all packed with boxes and furniture on top. He saw us coming, and he yelled at her.

"Git in! We're movin' now."

Mary's head jerked back as if to say no. Her mother sat in the car and hung her head in shame. Baby Dewey, her brother, stood up in the back seat wearing only a diaper. He waved his fat little hand at us.

"Bye Bye! Bye Bye!"

"Git. Now I said! Now or else!"

Mary's father had such an evil look on his face. It was blood red, and there seemed to be steam coming out of his nose. His nostrils flared open so wide that you could see the black hairs growing inside. He was a tall man with hands as big as a person's head, and I knew that if Mary didn't get in the car soon, he would come after her. A sick feeling came inside me, and my stomach began to feel upset. It was like I looked into a nightmare. Mary's father was squeezing her neck and pulling her hair so hard that some of her curls fell on the sidewalk. I stood holding Janey's hand, and a lump came into my throat. I couldn't speak.

"Now, you little heifer. Git your ass in this car! I'll strap the life outta ya' and no one can stop me. Do what I say bitch!"

His neck bulged, and the buttons on his plaid shirt seemed ready to fly off into the air any second. The smell of him was sickening. My head began to spin when his rotten odor hit me. Mary's daddy reached past my face and yanked her by the shoulder up off the ground. Her shoe, the one with the broken buckle, fell off and I picked it up in my hand. Mary needed her shoe! I began to follow them to the car. Mary's daddy was still holding her up in the air by her shoulder. Her neck was twisted around toward me in a weird position. It seemed like her body was moving in the direction of the car, but her face was staying with us. We could see the fear in her blue eyes.

"But Mary needs her shoe!"

I ran up to her daddy and tapped his arm. He reached back with his huge hand to put it around my neck and choke me.

"I'll take the shoe, little girl."

Mary's mother had been silent until then. When she spoke, it confused Mary's daddy. He took his hand from around my neck, and then he dropped Mary on the ground. She landed on the grass on her back. She hummed a little song that the nun taught us that first Saturday in May.

"On this day, oh beautiful Mother..."

Then my group of friends moved a little closer to Mary. Joe helped her up, and George picked her books up out of the dirt. Polly had wiped Mary's face. When Mary's daddy walked around to get in their car, Polly placed her own rosary around Mary's neck and tucked it down around her collar out of sight. Mary climbed into the back seat. When her daddy started the motor, we stood there by her door and said goodbye.

"Bye Mary. Remember Indianapolis!"

It began to rain as they drove away. I don't know where she went. I hope she found friends there. Maybe her daddy would die, and she would live happily ever after. She could go to school in peace and come home to care for baby Dewey. I knew it was bad to hope a person would die. I just thought that was the only way Mary and her family could have any peace. I was sorry to think that, but confused at the same time. We stood there in the rain. We were Mary's friends, and we walked home in silence that day.

Thirty-Three

Carry Me Home, I'm Your Captain

"Leave behind the things of the world, children! Leave the hate, the suffering, the injustices of man!"

I stood in the doorway of the new church on Delaware Street listening to the voice of the dark haired man.

"Oh, leave the decay of this dirty city! Come follow me now to the Promised Land."

A woman by the door led me to the back of the room and sat me down next to a young woman. I examined her dress out of the corner of my eye. The fabric was expensive, mint green and sewn into a short-sleeved design with a pleated skirt.

"Stop being concerned with exterior things! Do not the lilies of the field exist in all their natural splendor? Doesn't the One Being give us all we need?"

I watched as the woman next to me raised her arms up to the ceiling with each question from the man up on the stage.

"I say stop! Stop it now! Come follow me where no evil can come! I say come! Follow me! Now! I say come!"

The woman swayed, and her head bobbed up and down as she was suffering from some bad sickness. I heard her crying, wiping her face with a tiny decorated hanky. It had pink flowers all around the edges and each time, she picked out a spot in the middle of the hanky to dab her skin. It was like she was making herself ill. Then the next minute, she nursed herself back into calm. It was scary to see her, but I was too curious to look away.

"Oh Yeah! No evil can enter if you follow me now. Tomorrow, we will be in the land of the free, the home of the Holy One who waits for you and me!"

The woman shook and moaned, and I thought she was going to fall down.

"Amen! Come now. Rise. Go forward. Come to me children! I am your Father."

He was standing up there all alone, the man with the shiny black hair and the warm smile. His arms were stretched out, and people got out of their chairs to go and see him. One by one, they waited in line for him to touch their heads. Some folded their arms across their chests. Others clasped their hands tightly in fists of prayer. It was almost as if the people were going to receive Holy Communion. In the Catholic Church, I knew there was light and freedom. In the House of the Lord, we sang songs to the Father. But this church was different. No light came in the windows; no person had the peace of Christ in their eyes. They were blank people, faces looking but nothing to be seen in their eyes. There were no signs or symbols to remind me of Jesus.

This church was scary. There seemed to be a dark feeling hovering in the background. It was heavy, and I thought it was making the woman next to me sick. When I turned around, the feeling appeared as a cloud and floated in front of me. It landed above the heads of the people in front of me, but they didn't seem to notice it. The gray cloud then flew over and surrounded the preacher. Each person he touched became blurry to me. The sky was bright outside, but I began to shake with cold. As the wind came in and blew all around the inside, I held my hands together in prayer. I did not want to go up to the preacher, yet I couldn't see the way out. I knew the door was to the left of me. If I just rose up slowly and moved over, I could probably walk out. My body was heavy, and it seemed like I was glued to my chair. I folded my hands so tight that they hurt. It was painful to pray. I couldn't think of anything, and my time was running out. The woman next to me grabbed my shoulder and pushed me ahead of her in the line. I saw the thin wisps of the cloud swirl in front of me. It was a strange church, and I didn't want to go up to the preacher. I prayed that he wouldn't touch my head.

"Forward! Walk forward! Oh, you who seek the freedom from all pain!"

My stomach was churning inside as I got closer to the preacher. There were only two women ahead of me in the line. Then I thought I heard a voice calling my name.

"Emmie. Oh Emmie. Your mother is looking for you. Emmie! Emmie! Go with me now!"

Bernadette was standing in the doorway. The light shone all around her as she held out her hand. I ran out right before it was my turn to get my head touched by that minister. He had his hands extended to me, but Bernadette's voice was loud and clear.

"Your mother wants you now, Emmie."

I walked fast away from the black haired preacher and toward Bernadette in her long blue dress. The people moaned in their chairs as I passed by them, the ones who had their heads pressed with the preacher's hands. I could hear him speaking as I turned my back.

"Now we are all united. We are one family of brothers and sisters! One clan! Oh, now we will walk from here to Heaven. We will go out and leave this valley of death."

They were all humming a low tune. I turned and saw the black haired preacher. He sat with his head bowed down, and the dark cloud swirled all around him. It moved closer until it was completely surrounding him. He was inside it, and it was inside him.

"How did you know I was in there Bernadette?"

"Little Emmie! When I prayed the rosary this morning, I meditated on the sorrowful mysteries, of how Mary was so sad when her Son was put to death on the cross for all of us sinners. I saw Mary crying for her child, and I heard her say *"My other children are suffering."* So I walked and walked, not knowing who or what children were suffering. I saw this church, but there was no light shining out from the windows. I felt darkness within my soul as I came near. What kind of children are in there, I wondered? But you—I saw you from the doorway. You were the only one not yet touched by the darkness of that man."

"You said my mother wants me. What's wrong?"

"Not your earthly mother, your heavenly mother, Mary. She wants you to remain with her and not to be touched by the Evil One."

We walked home that spring day. The red and yellow tulips shot out of the ground, and sparrows flew with us. No wind blew like the cold wind that had made me shiver. Bernadette served me cinnamon tea at her house. Polly and her sisters let me try on their jewelry. They walked me home before it got dark. At the door, Bernadette again gave me a warning.

"Some say the Reverend Jim is a cult leader. People have given him all their money, their cars and their homes. You are safe now. Do not go back to the Reverend Jones. Pray without ceasing."

She hugged me and patted me on the back. I ran inside to see Mommy. I didn't want to tell her what happened because she would be scared.

"I'm home now. I've been to Bernadette's."

"Are you okay, Emmie? Are you sure you can watch your sisters?"

"It's nothing, Mommy. I'm just tired. I'll make Janey and Cissy some eggs."

Mommy left, and I sang Loretta Lynn songs to my sisters. I stood on the coffee table and pretended it was the stage. Loretta wore a sparkly blue chiffon dress. Her dark hair hung down far to her waist. The hairdresser had curled her hair into loose waves. Loretta's diamond earrings matched her necklace. When she raised her arm to the ceiling, everyone admired her smooth throat and shoulders. Those sad songs made people cry and sniff their noses. Some ladies wiped their eyes with a tissue.

"Loretta! Come back on stage, Loretta. Sing one more song for us. Please Loretta!"

We colored pictures on a cardboard box.

"It's a treasure chest, Emmie!"

Janey put all kinds of things inside it-a comb, a nickel and my holy card with the picture of the Baby Jesus.

"Don't lose my stuff Janey. Take good care of it. If you see a real tall guy with black hair, and he is a preacher named Reverend Jones, don't go near him. I'll take you to a good church, Saint Mary's, because that other one is not for us. Or we can go to the House of the Lord Church. Okay? Now be careful of strangers. Just because someone is smiling doesn't mean that they are nice."

Janey listened to my speech, and then she wanted to hear more.

"Emmie, how do you know if someone is good?"

"Because they do good things."

"And how do you know if a man is bad?"

"You silly! 'Cause he has dark clouds swirling around him, and you might get a scared feeling right in the middle of your chest."

"What if you are blind, Emmie? A girl at school is blind. How would she see black clouds around a bad man? What then? How? Why? What if?"

"Janey, even if you didn't have any eyes or ears, you could still FEEL if a man is bad. Your chest will hurt, and you'll get a scared thought in your mind INSIDE!"

Then Janey and I rocked Cissy to sleep and watched the Lawrence Welk program on TV. Janey practiced doing the polka. She told me to pretend she had on a red dress with bows. She twirled around and curtsied when the dance was over.

"Are there any bad things here now, Emmie?"

"Well, do you feel anything bad?"

"No. I just feel dizzy because I've been doing the polka. I'm happy now."

"Then there isn't anything bad here now because bad and good can't be in the same place at the same time. We're safe."

I covered my sisters with the fuzzy white blanket and turned on the lamp by my chair. The television stayed on without the sound. Cowboys rode across the desert. I picked up my crossword puzzle book. What is a six-letter word for a person who saves another? I thought and watched as the cowboy guided one of his sheep away from the wolves. He had a long stick that he used to turn the lost sheep around. The animal stood still as if frozen with the hungry wolf waiting in the nearby bushes. The cowboy prodded the sheep and even hit it lightly on the shoulder until the young animal turned to run back to the group. The man rescued the sheep. That's it-a six-letter word for someone who rescues another-SAVIOR. I filled in the last blank and my eyes were heavy. The cowboy rode away to keep herding his flock of sheep toward another pasture.

"My girlie! Are your sisters asleep yet?"

"Yes Mommy. We watched cowboy shows and Lawrence Welk."

"Then you were safe while I was gone."

"Yeah, there was nothing bad here tonight."

I slept on the floor next to Janey and Cissy. The street light shined in all night. We were safe. It was good to hear Mommy breathing. Nothing bad happened the rest of the night.

Thirty-Four

Voices Carry

O n the last day of school that year, our teacher made us stand up beside our desks.

"Class, shake hands with everyone. Tell each person that you enjoyed their company this year."

Polly reached over my desk and grabbed my hand. She had on a yellow band with white roses to hold her hair back from her face.

"Thank you, Emmie, friend and neighbor.

It has been a good school year."

Her smile was so wide, and she giggled a little, covering her mouth. I shook her hand with firmness like I'd read in Manners for Business and Social Occasions. I would have to return that book to the library soon. I had some nice words for Polly all my own.

"Polly, thanks for being friendly to me and letting me help you. Everyone should meet a person like you."

"Emmie, Emmie, Emmie, Emmie!"

It was Joe tapping me hard on the shoulder. I turned around, but I had to bend my head back to look up to him. He had grown so tall. When he first came to school, I could look him straight in the eye. That day, he looked down at me.

"Thank you for walking to school with me and for listening to my songs."

He grinned, and I think he winked real fast with one eye.

"Thank you, Joe, for all the gifts and the great food from your mom. And for taking care of me when I needed help some days."

He just kept patting me on the shoulder until George interrupted.

"I would like to thank you Emmie. You are a big help. You are smart. You teach me many things about school and life. Also English. You show me how to live in Indianapolis."

George bowed the way he usually did. He shook my hand very quickly, still talking.

"Thank you. Thank you. Thank you, Emmie."

"George, I want to thank you also. You are very good, and you like school. Now you can speak English better than last year. Keep learning!"

We shook hands with the entire group of students, saying a nice word to each one. I thought I heard someone say my name, but everyone was busy talking to another boy or girl. Then I noticed the empty desk behind me, the one where Mary sat for a few weeks. On the floor under the desk, a piece of paper stuck out just enough so that you'd have to look really hard to see it. All I saw was something white, and it caught my attention. While everyone was busy talking, I reached down and pulled out the paper. It was a note all folded up until it was the size of a stamp.

"Dear classmates, when you find this note, I will be gone. I will probably have to move away again. My Paw does not like it here. He has been very sick lately. Thank you for being friendly to me. Your city is very nice. I like school here. Your friend, Mary."

I read the note, and I was starting to fold it away when Mr. Ramsey caught me.

"What do we have here? Give me the note, Emmie."

I watched as he smiled and read it to himself. He handed it back to me.

"Please read this letter out loud, Emmie. Stand up here and face the class."

I walked to the front of the room and stopped for a second. I coughed.

Then I began to read the note from Mary. One little girl wiped her eyes with her hand. Another boy put his head down on his desk. When I finished reading, the silence was strong. I sat down in my seat, the children clearing their throats and some of them coughing just to fill up the air with sound. Joe got up and laid a paper on the desk that was Mary's. It was a picture of our school with a little blond girl out in front. She wore a name tag that said Mary. Joe was quick. He could draw a perfect picture in a minute. Mr. Ramsey passed the picture all around the class. Each one of us wrote our name and "Hi Mary" or "Thank you."

I wrote "From your friend in Indianapolis, Emmie O'Brien."

When he took the picture back from the last student, Mr. Ramsey looked at us.

"I don't know if the next school that Mary attends will ask for her records. If they do, I will send her this greeting from the class. Now go out and have a good summer. Keep safe and remember to be good."

He stood by the door as we filed out one by one. I was the last student to leave the room. I watched as he shook everyone's hand and patted them on the head as they passed by. I waited until the last moment.

"Thank you, Mr. Ramsey. You are a very good teacher."

"Oh Emmie! What a good student you are. Keep studying and reading always."

I turned and waved to Mr. Ramsey, and then he locked the classroom door. He went out the back door to the teachers' parking lot. All of the students walked down the front steps toward our homes in the neighborhood.

Thirty-Five

The Hands That Built America

I t was my thirteenth birthday. The whole neighborhood was up early
that July 4th. My family had a box packed with food, and I stood on the
porch ready to go. Joe and his family, mother, father, cousins, aunts, all
of them passed by our house on the way to University Park. Every one of
them carried a box or a cake pan wrapped in aluminum foil. Joe carried a
bucket with their potato salad and a ring of ice to keep it cold.

"Got your favorite peach butter, Sweetie Pie! Come get you a helpin' when
you're ready to eat." Joe's mama stuck out her hand and yelled as she walked
past.

"Have to keep goin' or all this'll go to ruin. Hope you join us."

I was dreaming of that thick orange stuff, the peach butter, and how it was
so stiff that your spoon always got stuck in the jar straight up. I ran back
inside.

"Hurry, Mommy, or we'll be late."

I went out to the sidewalk and spotted George and his family all in a
line. First George's father came carrying a bowl covered in wax paper and
wrapped in a towel. Mrs. Washington came next. Both her arms were
stretched around a metal soup pot with only two rags to protect her from

the heat. She was holding that pot like she didn't trust anyone else. George followed after his mother in the line. He carried a large glass jar of iced water and a cup for everyone to drink from. Grandma was the last person. She walked slowly behind the others. In one of her hands, she carried a canvas bag. She must have known how curious I was since she stopped and let me look inside it. The aroma of fish and vegetables came up toward me as I peeled back the white towel.

"Eggroll."

Those were the only words I could understand from her. She closed the towel over the food and smiled at me. A few of her front teeth were chipped, but she was pretty healthy. I imagined that she said to come and eat an egg roll at the park. All her other words were in Chinese, yet I think I knew what she meant. The family slowed down a little until Grandma joined the procession. Bernadette and her daughters marched down the street, each one carrying ceramic pots of food. Polly got out of line to talk to me.

"We are having spiced pork with noodles and cabbage. After that, we have cherry dumplings and drink cinnamon tea."

It all sounded so good, and I was eager to leave.

"We're going too, Polly, just as soon as Mommy's dressed."

I watched all the neighbors pass by heading for the park downtown. Mommy came out on the porch carrying Cissy. This time, Mommy had on her blue pedal pushers and her white blouse. She wore sneakers just like Janey and me. I helped Mommy load the box into the wagon. Janey pulled it for a while, but then we had to take turns. We headed downtown like the rest of the group. Cissy got to ride all the way.

The park near the World War Memorial building was full. Only a few people sat at tables. The rest of the families spread their tablecloths on the ground. Mommy found a picnic table under a tree right in the middle of the park. All our neighbors were sitting by us. Joe's family was over in a corner. George and his family were nearby. Polly and her family had a spot by Meridian Street. On the corner by Pennsylvania and Michigan Streets, a group of shopkeepers and their families had a place. They had carried a folding table and chairs to the park. I saw Mr. Steinbaum, the meat store man, and his wife set up a big tray of barbecued chicken. The drugstore owner, Mr. Farmer, dumped bags of corn chips and pretzels into a metal bucket until they overflowed. The supermarket man, Mr. Allen, stirred a kettle full of white beans and ham. The man who owned the bowling alley had washtubs with cold bottles of root beer and cream sodas on ice. The museum guard and his wife set out a platter of cornbread and butter. Miss Andrea, the librarian who always helped us, cooked a giant meatloaf in a pan she had borrowed from the hospital. Her sister Sara worked in the cafeteria, and said they could return the pan before anyone noticed it was missing. Mommy's friend Alice brought jars of homemade sweet pickles and spiced pears. You should have seen the salad that the Pastor of The House of the Lord sat out. He and his wife made the most beautiful arrangement of chopped eggs and tomatoes on shredded lettuce and olives. They even had a jar of their own Italian Cream dressing.

"Emmie, stop dreaming! Set this casserole on the table. It's our macaroni and ham with Cheddar cheese. Don't drop it. Be careful with my fried chicken."

I took the pan from Mommy and placed it next to the salad.

"Here, Emmie, since you are the set-up girl, take these peanut butter cookies and this fudge."

Mrs. Santoni and Mrs. O'Leary had walked to the park together since they were friends and their husbands had long since died. They were widows. Mr. Ramsey and his family smiled at me then went to put their bacon- wrapped hot dogs and chili sauce on the table. My teacher looked different without his white shirt and tie. He was wearing a light blue shirt and some of the buttons were undone at the neck. He didn't have on his tie. How strange he looked out of the classroom.

Polly and her sisters came to set their food on the table. They found a spot next to the egg rolls and the Washington family's shrimp and rice. Mr. Clark, the tavern owner where Mommy worked, brought boxes of buns and gallon jars of peanuts and pepperoni sticks. The ladies who worked at the Laundromat donated napkins and apples. Some of the sisters from St. Mary's were the last to arrive at the park. They came hurrying, rustling their long black habits and swinging their arms back and forth. Sister Felicia winked at me. I was admiring her wooden rosary beads that hung from her belt. I knew she remembered me from the first Saturday in May, the day when little Mary crowned our Mother Mary, and we all knelt with her in prayer. Sister Felicia let out a sigh and said a remark to anyone listening.

"It's a great day the Lord has brought us together. All thanks and praise!"

The other nuns set a huge chocolate cake at the end of the table. The cake was four layers thick and baked on a metal tray from the church kitchen. One of the nuns sprinkled chopped pecans on the top and cherries. Some people nearby stared at that cake. It was enough to feed fifty people.

"Oooh! Mmmm!"

A crowd was beginning to form around the cake. Pastor Penning clapped his hands to get our attention.

"Silence. Silence. Please."

The people stopped talking and waited. His voice became louder, and the crowd quieted down.

"We are gathered here this Fourth of July to celebrate our unity. All of us here are brothers and sisters in this, the greatest country in the world. Each of us is free today while others in the world are kept in prisons. They are tortured for speaking out against evil and prevented from knowing true peace and brotherly love. Let us never forget to keep our eyes open to injustice, and never let the evil spirit of apathy rule our homes, our minds, or our land. It is a terrible spirit-never seeing, never knowing and never caring, and it makes its way through the world. Never give up. Fight strong with the holy spirits of love and patriotism and never forget the Greatest One of All. God Bless America!"

The people joined in and added their own words.

"Amen!"

"Uh huh!"

"Right on!"

"You said it man!"

"U.S.A!"

"Land of the free! Home of the brave!"

They all said something.

"And keep our city beautiful!"

Everyone stared at me when I said that. Up until then, the speech was all about America and the world. But the city where I lived was part of the celebration also. One woman laughed then another joined in. They were from the nurses' bowling league.

"God bless Indianapolis," I added.

They clapped and patted me on my back. All the people in the food line told me what a great idea it was to bless the city. They looked directly at me when they talked like I was some older person.

"You gotta start small. Work up to big things."

"Maybe the Lord wants us to work on one city at a time."

"This is a good city, isn't it?"

I thought about their comments as I looked up. The sun was high above Lady Victory's head. We were so close to the monument. I could see her raising her arm proud up high to heaven. The air was still, and I could hear a dove call in the distance. People were quiet now, just starting to get their food. The bells rang out from Christ Church Cathedral on the Circle. We were close enough to hear the noon bells. For a few seconds, all was silent except the sound of a bird's wings. It was a long space of time. People moved their mouths, but I didn't hear any of their words. A light came over the park and made everything brighter. It was a beautiful light, rosy pink and full of goodness. I turned my head to see where the light was coming from. But it was just like when it rains where you're standing, and everywhere around you is dry. You stand under the falling drops and get wet, and then a few feet in front of you, there's the dry part. But we weren't wet. This light was just there, not coming from anywhere. The light was just there.

I began to notice that the people who had caused me trouble weren't there. Mr. Ogre. The big ugly man who snuck in and tried to grab my sisters and me. The demon who attacked Polly. Johnny who tried to hurt me and force his way into me. The gang of boys. The witch women. The man who killed little Billy's daddy. That preacher with those black clouds swirling all around him. That drunk old monster who took our pretty friend Mary and baby

Dewey away. That mean boy from school who ridiculed my friends. The vodka and whiskey and those little black pills. Maybe they weren't invited. Maybe the neighborhood prayed for them to stay away.

Everyone started talking louder. The picnic began. Each person brought their own plate and silverware. Janey and I had to borrow a fork from Polly because we forgot ours. I went back in line to get another helping and that's when I spotted Joe's mama's biscuits. They were still warm as I spread peach butter on top. I stood in line and ate two of them right on the spot. I was sure to try a small portion of every item on the table.

"Freedom. We have freedom."

George's father walked by me with a chunk of cornbread dripping with butter. He licked his fingers and then patted his heart.

"Because we have freedom in the U.S.A., I have freedom in myself."

He walked away from me, laughing, whistling and saluting the flag flying high up on the pole.

I sat down next to Mommy and her friend Sonny. He got out his guitar and sang a song about me.

"Oh EMMIE, Oh EMMIE, she's from Indianapolis. Her hair is dark red and her eyes are so brown. Oh EMMIE, Oh EMMIE, she paints at the museum. She sings at the church and she studies at school.

OH EMMIE, OH EMMIE, she walks 'round the Circle. She draws pretty pictures and writes all day long. She loves her sisters and bakes oatmeal cookies. And everyone knows her in the whole blessed town!"

Cissy danced in her bare feet on the grass. Sonny sang and strummed his guitar. He propped one of his black cowboy boots, the ones with the white stars, on the bench. He wore that white shirt with his black leather vest that I loved. With his other foot, he tapped on the ground. When Sonny finished each verse, he placed a harmonica in his mouth. He made the same tunes as the guitar, but no words for that part. Cissy started to sing.

"Oh EMMIE, Oh EMMIE, my sister downtown."

We all clapped when Cissy stopped singing. Those were the most words that she'd ever said and they were a song.

Thirty-Six

Somebody to Love

I left Mommy for a while to go visit Daddy. He was standing to the side of the park on New York Street. There was a new red Volkswagen parked next to him.

"Hey, look at my new car."

He looked really happy that day. His black hair was cut short on top, and he was wearing a new green shirt, one of those pullover ones with a row of buttons at the neck.

"Is it really yours, Daddy?"

"All mine and yours."

Daddy's new Volkswagen was shiny red, like an apple all polished and setting there at the curb.

"You are going to live with me now. Go and get your sisters, and we'll go to our new house."

I had to think for a few minutes. There was Lady Victory. I loved to gaze at her. She was facing south, her back towards us as she kept watch over the enemies of war, preventing their terrible force from overcoming the city. She was welcoming the soldiers home from the war. Around me, I heard the children playing. They called out, "You're it!" They giggled as they ran around the oak trees.

"Emmie! Come play hide and seek."

Polly's voice called out to me. It became stronger and louder until all my friends dragged me away from my father. I ran around every tree in the park and down every path, but I couldn't catch anyone to tag them. Just as I was getting dizzy from running so much, I fell down in front of Joe's family. I was lying there on my back, and I couldn't get up. A few clouds rolled by until a big form came to rest by my shoulders. Joe's mama leaned over me and pulled me up with her strong hands right into the center of her chest. Her arms squeezed me tight until I felt like my breath was coming back into my body.

"Whatever's the matter child? What's gotten ahold of you now?"

When I got my head to stop spinning, and I was sure my feet were not moving, I told her.

"Daddy has a new red car, and we're moving back with him!"

"Wonderful! And where you movin' to, girl?"

"To the south side."

Mrs. Dorster squeezed me so hard that all I could do was smell the aroma of buttermilk biscuits. It seemed like the smell came out of the skin on her neck. She had my face pressed down into her bosom, and she wouldn't let me go. I began to feel stronger every minute. Over her shoulder, I saw that plate of biscuits piled high on the serving table. I was thinking that as soon as she let me go, I'd ask her to fix me one with more peach butter. Finally, she unwrapped her arms from around me and stood me up. I didn't fall down.

"That was a Love Hug. So you won't ever forget me. Now I know one little girl will love me on the south side. That's all I need. Just one little girl to love me!"

"Thank you, Mrs. Dorster."

I spoke quietly, but I knew she heard me when I added "Mama" after my words. I knew because she winked at me and handed me one of her big biscuits like I'd been hoping for.

"Here, Precious. You know your Mama wouldn't let you go without a little

162

something to eat."

I walked away stuffing the flakes of the biscuit into my mouth and licking all the peach butter that had dripped on my hands. When they were clean, I blew her a kiss. How joyful she looked, bouncing up and down.

Thirty-Seven

As Time Goes By

I almost ran into the little group where George and his parents played a card game. As I got closer, I saw that they were flash cards with letters. They were spelling out words in English. I stooped down and took the rest of the deck from the ground. They were big white cards, the size of a paperback book, and I laid each black symbol out in a row. The family gathered around my word, bending their heads and thinking hard. I wanted them to keep playing the game, and I watched as they whispered and pointed. George was the first to read what I had written on the ground.

"Goodbye?"

I shook my head yes.

"Where are you going, Emmie?" George was speaking English very well. "Perhaps on a vacation?"

He kept trying to guess where I was going. Then George's father took my right hand in both of his making it impossible for me to escape.

"Our little friend is going on a journey. Her goodbye is a word of permanence not said lightly."

Mr. Washington then told us a story.

"There was a young deer that left the group of animals with whom he had been raised. He wandered away and joined another group in a different part of the forest. He had a happy life. When he became old, he began to think of the other animals, and he missed them. Since he could never see his friends again, the old deer told stories about them to the young deer. In that way, the animals from the old group, in the other part of the forest, became alive again. So he spent his days remembering the time of his youth. And if you pass through certain parts of the forest, you can hear the young deer laughing and crying out.

"Please Grandfather Deer, tell us the story of when you lived in the other part of the forest before you came to live with us. Tell us how it used to be when you were young."

Mrs. Washington stood quietly beside her husband and lowered her head at the end of the story. Grandma then took hold of me. She placed her hands on my head and pressed hard, muttering something in Chinese. Mr. Washington translated her words for me.

"She says that you must remain unchanged wherever you go. Do not allow evil eyes to pierce into your skull. Laugh at stones when they are thrown at your body. Always carry a piece of paper in your pocket on which to write your final confession of life."

There were flags flying everywhere that day-the state flag of Indiana, the United States flag and the flag of Indianapolis, the Crossroads of America. They flew high on top of the Federal Building, waving when a breeze passed by. My little friend George saluted me.

"I speak English now. I am George Washington of Indianapolis, Indiana and the United States of America. Earth. The Universe."

They all stood there in a row, George and his parents and Grandma. They saluted me. As I walked away, I saluted them also.

"And I am Emmie of Indianapolis."

George and his family bowed to me. I walked backward away from them because I didn't want to leave. I didn't want to turn around.

Thirty-Eight

She's Leaving Home

B ernadette caught me as I walked backward. I fell on a rock, landing right in the middle of her blanket. Polly and her sisters gathered around me.

"Okay? You are fine now?"

Polly worried and clasped her hands together.

"Emmie? You hurt? Is your head good? Yes? Yes?"

Her sisters asked me various questions to see whether I was conscious and made me answer one by one.

"Where are you?"

"What holiday is today?"

"What color is your hair?"

"Who is Santa Claus?"

This went on until I'd satisfied Polly's sisters.

"I am Emmie. I have two little sisters and my mother and father. I'm at University Park in Indianapolis, Indiana. This is the Fourth of July. Today is my birthday, and I'm thirteen years old now. My hair is red, and I like the Beatles, Paul McCartney best of all. Santa Claus brings gifts to girls and boys on Christmas if they are good. I want a guitar. My favorite movie is The Wizard of Oz. I'm a Catholic. My favorite food is coconut meringue pie that my mother makes. My hobbies are reading, drawing, baking, singing, and daydreaming. I want to be a teacher when I grow up, or a nun, or maybe a singer. I love my family and my friends. I want to travel and go to Russia someday. China. The world. Are there any more questions?"

Each girl nodded her head and smiled when I said the correct answer. They took turns rubbing my head and examining me for lumps or bleeding. They touched my forehead to see if I had a fever, made me drink a glass of hot tea. One listened to my heart, one took my pulse, and another peered into my eyes. They checked my back to see if it was bleeding, and one of them rubbed Romanian Dreams Beauty Cream on my temples to soothe me.

"You have good health. Nothing hurts your head. Now stand up to receive your fortune and your blessing."

Bernadette pulled me up to my feet where I stood in the center of her family. Polly came forward with her pronouncement.

"You will know many good hours. Some bad."

The women in turn stepped closer to me. They laid their hands on my shoulders and told me their thoughts.

"You will be a friend."

"You will be honest."

"You will guard the things in your heart."

When they finished, I had many blessings from Polly and her sisters. As Bernadette moved forward, I felt heat coming with her and filling my body all the way to my fingers and my toes. It was a happy type of warmth, and I waited eagerly for her pronouncement. She took her time. The sound of her words came slowly toward me.

"Look at these hands."

Bernadette reached for my hands and turned my palms face up.

"Whatever you do with these hands must be good. Never do evil with them. Do not permit the works of the evil one to be performed through these hands. Accept only money that has been earned or rightly given you to be placed in them. Eat what is good and drink what is clean with the help of your hands.

Hold babies, touch only your husband, and make beautiful works with them. Read wonderful books. Paint colorful pictures and write only what benefits those who read your words. Never allow letters of contempt to leave your house, and wash your windows so that the sun can shine in. If a book of destruction comes to lie upon your lap, throw it fast onto the garbage pile. Most of all, clasp your hands in prayer each day so that you will continue to receive the graces of God the Father. Amen."

Bernadette slowly let go of my hands. She stepped back until I was left standing alone on the blanket. Polly and her sisters surrounded me.

"You are leaving?"

Polly must have known, but I hadn't told her yet.

"I'm moving out of the neighborhood to the south side with my dad and my little sisters. Mommy's going to stay here and go to secretary school."

They all began to hug and kiss me, wiping their eyes and moaning.

Bernadette was the last to embrace me.

"Whenever a friend comes, we are happy. When a friend is here, we are rich while they are visiting us. When a friend leaves, we are sad. When our friend is gone, we are rich again with their memory."

I hugged her around the waist. She wasn't very tall, and I had grown a few inches since I met her.

"Thank you, Bernadette, for teaching me and giving me lots of candy from your store. Thanks for letting me wear your jewelry and your hats and for giving me the rosary."

This time, I walked away in the right direction, forward. I did turn slightly. I waved and blew kisses to Polly and her family. I kept walking ahead until I reached Mommy. She was sitting at our table smoking a cigarette. The smell of the menthol cleared my head, and I sat down on the bench across from her. I waited a few minutes before I told her.

"Daddy says we're going to live with him. Janey and Cissy will be okay. I'll take care of them while you go to business classes at the college. Daddy has a new house with three bedrooms. I'll have my own. The walls are pink, and I have a pink bedspread with white curtains. I have my own closet and desk. Janey and Cissy have bunk beds. Cissy's going to sleep on the bottom so she won't fall out on the floor in the middle of the night. We have wall-to-wall carpet and window fans. Daddy has a new stove from Sears. I can bake cakes and pies. I can put up my posters of the Beatles and Sonny and Cher. I'll be in junior high. I get to join the Art Club and sing in the choir, probably Home Economics too. Daddy's taking me shopping at J.C. Penney's for a corduroy jumper, suede boots and a leopard print purse. I need some new glasses because I can't see the blackboard very well."

Mommy reached across the table to pat my hand.

"We can visit you on Sundays, if you want us to."

She started crying, so I hugged her.

"When I graduate, I'll make more money, and we can be together, honey. We'll ride the train to Florida and eat lobster by the ocean."

"Don't worry Mommy, we'll call you. You can say Hi to Cissy. Alice lives close by."

Sonny played his guitar real low, humming as if he were far away from us. Janey and Cissy came over to kiss Mommy. She held them for a long time.

"I will be healthy, and I won't smoke so many cigarettes. I'll try to cut down on my drinking. I'll make fried chicken for you on Sundays.

Mommy combed Cissy's hair and gave her a little drink of warm coffee with sugar. She smacked her lips, and Mommy kissed them. It was funny to see, but I didn't feel funny.

"Go with your Daddy, girls. He's waiting for you."

Mommy let us go, and we yelled to her.

"Bye Mommy!"

"Love you Mama"

"See you Sunday!"

"Love ya girls!"

"Mom, we will all be okay," I told her.

Thirty-Nine

The Long and Winding Road

❧⁓⁓❧

I took Janey and Cissy by the hand, and we walked over to where Daddy was waiting by our new car. All the kids at the picnic gathered around us. Daddy could only pick three of them to take a ride around town. We got in and put Cissy in the back window since she was so little. Janey sat on my lap in the front. Joe and George and Polly were chosen by Daddy to ride in the back seat.

"You get in. And you! Hey girl, hurry. Watch your skirt in the door."

Daddy shut the door and started the motor. The Volkswagen sputtered and lurched forward out of the parking spot and into the street. Cissy waved to everyone from the window. Daddy honked the horn and drove away. Around and around the Circle, he drove us. We yelled and waved at the people who were walking around.

"Happy Fourth of July!"

"America the Beautiful!"

"Hey Lady Victory!"

We called out to everyone while Daddy drove us around the city. He pointed out buildings and named all the cars and the trees. Once more around the Circle, then Daddy drove us back to the park. He opened the door for my friends to get out. Polly and George and Joe stood by the side of the car. They talked to me through the window.

"We'll miss you, Emmie."

Polly took off her crucifix, the one she brought from Romania, and leaned through the window to hang it around my neck. Joe shook his head next.

"Who will I walk to school with and who'll listen to me sing?"

He reached down into his pocket and took out something. It was a piece of birch tree bark where he had written *"EMMIE"* with a heart around it. I took the bark and thanked him.

"I'll never forget you, Joe."

George came over and handed me an Indianapolis Times newspaper. He pointed to a letter to the editor written by George's father. He wrote about his family escaping from China and how grateful they were for helpful friends in the city.

"You are a friend. God bless you."

"God bless you, too, George."

"Bye everyone! I will miss you! You are all my friends! I'll see you someday again. Don't forget about me!"

I could see all the parents and the other people from the neighborhood standing in a group. They waved as Daddy pulled away from the curb. He drove around the park, honking the horn on our new red Volkswagen. Mommy blew us kisses and waved as we turned the corner. When I looked back, everyone got smaller and smaller until all I could see was a mass of people. They were all colors and clothing and hair and jewelry gathered around the table as if they were painted in a picture. Then we left, and that picture entered into my mind forever.

Forty

Acknowledgments

I want to dedicate this book to the Holy Family-Jesus, Mary and Joseph. My husband Tony and my son Richard. My father Edward who always said "Keep On." My mother, Mary, who set an example for me with her letter-writing. My sisters Josie and Susan. My big brother Tom. My family and friends. My teachers who encouraged me to write. The countless characters inside the stories I've read. And the most beautiful city in the world, Indianapolis.

Forty-One

About the Author

K ay Castaneda is a retired English teacher. Her articles about education and sociology are included in Sage Publication's Education and Society Reference Book. Her poetry and creative nonfiction have been published in literary journals. Kay is currently researching her family history in Ireland, in addition to editing her poetry manuscript.

Kay attended Summer Literary Seminar's workshop in Vilnius, Lithuania. She also attended writing workshops at the University of Edinburgh in Scotland and San Miguel Allende, Mexico. She lives in Mexico with her husband Tony, son Richard and dogs Whitey and Buddy. Kay's hobbies include reading, writing, genealogy, traveling and visiting flea markets.

Emmie of Indianapolis is Kay's first novel.

Thanks for reading! Please add a short review on Amazon and let me know what you thought! Subscribe to my newsletter to get news and updates from me. Thank You!

https://mailchi.mp/2ca4d4d34805/newsletter-sign-up

https://www.goodreads.com/author/show/13851635.Kay_Castaneda

https://www.bookplaces.blog

https://www.facebook.com/Kaycastaneda90

https://www.twitter.com@kcastanedauthor

https://www.instagram.com/Kaycastaneda90

email kay@whiteriverwriters.com

Afterword

"Without memory, there is no culture. Without memory, there would be no civilization, no society, no future."

Elie Wiesel